I0673411

Dead Things

LT KoDZo

Dead Things

© 2015,2020 by LT Kodzo. All rights reserved.

Published by Kodzo Books, www.kodzobooks.com.

All rights reserved. No part of this book may be reproduced, stored in a retrieval system, or transmitted in any form or by any means – electronic, mechanical, photocopy, recording, or otherwise – without written permission of the author, except for brief quotations in printed reviews.

Cover design by Rocío Martín Osuna

ISBN: 978-1-943960-79-8

UTE TERMS

Maiku (my-kuh): Hello

Nuchu (new-chew): The people

Ouray (ooo-ray or you-ray):
   Arrow, also the name of a Ute Chief

Pyen (pay-yan): Mom

Paa (pa): Water

Uinta (you-in-tah):
   Natural Features (e.g. rivers, mountains)

Uintah (you-in-tah):
   Possibly a political term for natural features (e.g. county or reservation)

Ute (yoot):
   A tribe of North American Indians living in Utah and Colorado.

.

CHAPTER 1

Q: *What does the word dinosaur mean?*
A: *Terrible lizard.*

"I love dead things."

The noise in the classroom stopped.

The PowerPoint presentation behind Jimmy illuminated the dim room in a creepy blue.

His tenth-grade English teacher frowned at him. She probably thought he was going to talk about zombies or ghosts or something dumb. But he wasn't. Jimmy actually did love dead things.

The real dead.

The decayed and silent and harmless dead.

He cleared his throat to continue, but Mrs. Harris stopped him before he could say another word.

"Tell us your name," the teacher said.

Jimmy rolled his eyes. He hated the introduction ritual, not just because it was stupid, but because he didn't like his full name. James Hunter was his father's name, and Jimmy wanted nothing to do with that dead, white man. But he currently had a bigger problem facing him. In order to get out of the F-zone in English, he had to finish his two-hundred-word, oral essay.

He bit the inside of his lip. Not a single student smiled at him. A couple kids refused to even make eye contact. He tossed his long, black braid over his shoulder and asked, "Do I get all of my points if I start over?"

Mrs. Harris squinted at him before addressing the entire class. "I will make this one exception, but you all know better. I've told you all year how important it is to introduce yourself during public speaking events. I will dock anyone else five points if I have to remind you again."

To emphasize her point, she jabbed her index finger toward a couple of boys in the back. One of them whispered, "great," while the other flipped Jimmy off from under his desk.

Whatever. Making his bullies angry didn't matter. He didn't prepare his "I Love Blank" assignment for them anyway. He did it for his grade. Parent-teacher conferences were in two days and Pyen wouldn't like that he was failing English. Not that his mother would do anything harsh. She left that task up to whatever white boyfriend she had at the time. She always blabbed to them about him.

"We're waiting." Mrs. Harris tapped her pencil on the clipboard.

The class laughed. That didn't bother Jimmy either. When you weigh over two-hundred-fifty pounds at sixteen years old, you get used to laughs. Instead, Jimmy stood up tall and cleared his throat.

"My name is James Hunter." He barfed out the hideous title, then added the facts everyone already knew. "I'm a sophomore at Fife High in Puyallup, Washington, and I'd like to present my oral essay titled 'I Love Dead Things'."

He glanced at the teacher and she nodded. A girl in the front row leaned forward and pulled long sleeves over bruised wrists. Jimmy didn't know her, but he recognized the reason for winter flannel while the rest of the school embraced spring in summer shorts. He advanced the presentation. "According to Merriam-Webster, the word 'dead' means something is no longer alive.

"It can no longer feel. It can no longer move. Therefore, it can no longer hurt you."

He exhaled. Thirty-two words done, one-hundred-sixty-eight to go. While he was used to being fat, he still didn't like standing exposed to the critical eyes of his classmates.

He clicked to the next slide where an animated, screaming T. rex appeared to climb into the room. "The Tyrannosaurus rex has historically been labeled one of the most ferocious animals to ever walk on land, yet since extinction, his reputation has changed."

The next page showed images of Barney, plus the horse-like T. rex from the Age of Zombies and the quirky smiles of monsters turned friendly in the old TV show Dinosaurs. Jimmy talked about how most people didn't even know that the word dinosaur meant terrible lizard. "Their ability to entertain has replaced the true facts related to them.

"While some modern re-creators of this savage beast captured its real desire to kill and destroy"—Jimmy clicked through images from the movie Jurassic Park, and the game Minecraft and a screenshot of Grimlock from Transformers— "the real question is, why would anyone choose to change the idea of something so vicious and present it as tamable?"

He looked around the classroom. Kids that sometimes snickered at him were paying attention. Cool. He exhaled again and shifted his weight from one sore foot to the other. This was actually working out for him. After spending a life studying death, he found a place where his childhood experience proved useful. He swallowed and said, "Dead things are safe things." He looked directly at the front-row girl. "The dead no longer have the ability to hurt the living."

He clicked to a pic of a museum with the skeletal remains of frozen beasts.

"They are quiet."

He clicked on an image of an old lady putting flowers into the mouth of a T. rex vase.

"They are tamed."

He clicked on his favorite picture and smiled. The green-painted monster that monitored downtown Vernal, Utah. The statue, two states away, was dressed in a cowboy hat eating a gigantic watermelon. He loved this corny image for two reasons. It validated that the dead were honestly tamed, and because it stood only twenty-five miles down the highway from the Uintah and Ouray Reservation where his mother was born.

"In our world today, dinosaurs are fun. You can't say that about most living animals until long after they are dead." He hadn't written the report for the girl on the front row or anyone else like her, but he desperately wanted her to hear and understand. Her situation had a solution. He cleared his throat. "So, next time you visit a cemetery or a museum, consider how quiet and calm it is and remember, the dead always rest in peace."

The End appeared on the screen only to be eaten by an animated clip-art T. rex.

Mrs. Harris prompted the other tenth graders to clap. Jimmy felt his brown cheeks warm as he squeezed his way back to his desk. It was over and nothing bad happened. Until, of course, he sat down.

Plastic crunched beneath his butt.

Crap.

Girl-like giggles came from the boys behind him.

He smelled the applesauce before he felt the broken snack-pack seep through his stretch pants. He placed his hand on the desk and stared forward. The only way these boys would win with this prank was if he acknowledged that it happened. Instead he sat there without shifting through six other presentations until the bell rang. He'd kept a spare pair of sweats in his locker since freshman year. He refused to let a couple glee-geeks steal this moment from him.

Besides, now that the worst part of his day was over, he started to think about the worst part of his night.

Anxiety crawled around in his gut as the rest of the students filed from the class. In less than an hour, he'd be just another young Indian trying to survive in the white man's world.

CHAPTER 2

Q: *How did dinosaurs become extinct?*
A: *There seems to be as many answers to this
question as there are types of dinosaurs.*

The quiet afternoon lied to Jimmy. The calm of an empty house when he got home and the peace of doing homework without having to deal with Drunk Dean was a set-up. It provided Jimmy with no warning signs.

Which was why when the smoke alarm went off at 2:06 a.m., it yanked him from rare REM sleep he seldom enjoyed. Jimmy punched the mattress with his fist. His bedroom was appropriately dark, but the light from under the door validated his guess. The stupid white man was in the kitchen.

Come on.

Jimmy pushed his face into the pillow. Didn't that idiot know what time it was? Pyen's shift wouldn't end until 5:00 a.m. and Jimmy's Trig teacher wouldn't give a rat's behind that his mother's drunk boyfriend couldn't make eggs and bacon without waking the dead. And nothing in the world would make Mr. Ryan postpone a planned exam.

Jimmy flipped his long black braid over his shoulder and flopped onto his other side. A beam from a streetlight pushed through a gap in the curtain. Mounds of abandoned clothes created lumpy shadows around the floor. The slash of light revealed the sharp teeth on his T. rex poster. Just what he needed. Violent beasts baring their teeth at him. He took a balled-up sock and threw it at the monster for effect.

More sounds penetrated the apartment walls. Jimmy tightened his fist. No one should live this way. He never hated his mother's boyfriend more. Banging pots and curses collided through the darkness. Until, crash!

The screeching alarm stopped.

Pans clattered.

Drunk Dean probably used a baseball bat to disarm the alarm.

Idiot. Jimmy stuffed a pillow over his head. Please, just let that be the end of it. He wanted to sleep and forget all about his messed-up life, but the relief to his ears opened up his nose. Now he needed to push away the unwelcome smell of bacon. He didn't become fat without a healthy love for sizzling pork. But the idea of eating with Drunk Dean trumped his craving. This particular boyfriend had never hit him, but the six-foot-four-inch man reminded him of his father. Both were white and liked their alcohol mixed with temper.

He faced the wall and tightened his jaw. He thrust his desire for a slice of greasy bacon as far away from his nose and ears and eyes as possible. He didn't want to think about food, or about white men who like to date and marry, then abuse Indians. Tell you what, he didn't want to think about anything.

Fat chance.

Behind him, his door slammed open.

"You 'wake?" Drunk Dean slurred.

A rectangle of yellow light plastered the wall.

Jimmy stiffened. He never knew, on any given day, what might happen. Drunks were genuinely unpredictable. If Drunk Dean planned to hit him, he could prepare to defend himself, but if the man wanted a hug, being defensive only made things worse. The only thing he could count on with white men was nothing. Frickin' volatile.

"Want some breakfast?" The heaviness of alcohol weighed down the words.

Jimmy didn't move. His mother wouldn't be home for hours. Not that she'd help.

"Get up and—" Drunk Dean must have tried to walk into the room because the sentence ended with a thump near the floor, followed by angry swearing.

"Fat slob," the man yelled and kicked the bed frame.

I'm solid. I'm solid. I'm solid.

A book crashed against the wall at the foot of the bed. He prepped for whatever projectile came next and started his other mantra, Dad's dead, Dad's dead, Dad's dead.

"I know you're awake, you lazy pig."

Drunk Dean's tantrum continued with a barrage of socks and fast-food containers. Other guys Jimmy's age might have gotten up to fight. But he knew better. Best to let the soft parts of his body protect the parts that could break. He didn't earn the nickname Paa for nothing. The Ute Indian word for water accurately described his ability to flow or freeze depending on the temperature of the violence around him.

He flinched as a pair of jeans landed near his face. Thankfully, Dean couldn't find anything lethal to throw. After a balled-up T-shirt bounced against the covers, the man whined, "I'm just trying to be nice."

Jimmy sighed. He wanted to believe him. Wanted his mother's boyfriend to be different than the others. But there was no way he could even hope for that. Whether it was the alcohol, or part of the man's nature, that caused all the trouble, Jimmy needed to continue to pretend sleep. And for a big handful of time, he lay in bed and listened as Drunk Dean stumbled out of the room, dragging the rectangle of light with him as he closed the door.

Outside, the white man shouted, "Useless, fat half-breed."

"Drop dead," Jimmy whispered. He began tossing and kicking the jeans and T-shirt and junk off his bed. He threw back the covers and exhaled. The T. rex continued to snarl. White men were no different than dinosaurs. Dangerous. Violent. Better off dead. The noise in the other room evaporated. Studying the light under the door, Jimmy's full weight sunk into the mattress.

That's it. Nothing more to do tonight than forget about what just happened and use the PTSD coping skills he learned from his counselor. "The hypotenuse is the long, slanty side of a right triangle," he whispered into the sheet. "The adjacent side is next to the angle. The last side is called opposite." He yawned. "Sine is the ratio between the opposite and hypotenuse. Cosine is ..." His jaw relaxed.

Sleep must have overtaken him, because the next thing he knew, the thick taste of smoke choked his throat.

CHAPTER 3

Q: *Could dinosaurs breathe fire?*
A: *Most scientists doubt the concept of fire-breathing*
animals, but the idea exists in historical and mythical text.

Jimmy coughed only to find himself exhaling better air than he inhaled. Oh, crap. He opened his eyes then quickly closed them against the sting. What the ...

He flipped the covers off his body and tumbled to the floor, searching for air. A thick layer of smoke squirmed in the band of light above him. The greasy smell from before was gone. Now he tasted the grit of it. The apartment was on fire.

Crap, crap, crap.

The red glowing numbers from his alarm clock indicated only 45 minutes had passed since the smoke alarm first sounded. But there was no shrieking warning now. Instead, fire crackled and popped from beyond his closed door. This couldn't be happening. Where was Drunk Dean? Where was Pyen? He climbed over clothes toward his door. They're safe. They're safe. They're safe.

The smoke made it more than hard, but he crawled toward the door. The journey erased the heaviness of sleep. His brain remembered that his mother would still be at work. Her boyfriend, on the other hand, was probably passed out in the other room. The other room that, by the way, pushed smoke under his door.

Drop dead. Had he really said it?

Jimmy shook his head. It was wrong. No matter how bad a person was, a good person should never wish death on them. Especially not Jimmy. He knew his history. He knew his capacity to kill with words. The thought of Drunk Dean dying haunted him as he reached for the door handle.

"Ow."

He released the searing metal.

"Dean!" He shouted, then choked and gagged. Not again. He held back his fears. This can't be happening. One day without death. Just one day. Was that too much to ask? Come on, it followed him into the lives of all the men Pyen loved and lost. Jimmy didn't have the strength to deal with being responsible for another one. He just couldn't.

A loud crash in the other room forced him back like a defensive end. He crab-crawled over piles of dirty clothes until he was far enough away from the door to breathe. Although he'd lived with abusive white men most of his life, Jimmy felt more trapped at this moment than he could remember. All the other deaths had been so distant. But right now, only a few feet separated him from death. Beyond the bedroom door, Drunk Dean probably lay passed-out on the couch being consumed by fire. But Jimmy couldn't enter that room without killing himself too. The only chance of saving his victim was to move in the opposite direction. If his mother's drunk boyfriend wasn't already dead, the only way to rescue him was to get through the window. He had to tell someone.

He turned and crawled toward the gap in the curtains. Discarded junk slowed his progress, but it didn't stop him. In less than a second, he'd cleared stuff away and shoved open the window.

The moist night air fought its way to him and provided immediate relief. Yes. The crisp scent of spring promised Trig class would still take place tomorrow. A stupid thought, but he allowed it to encourage him. He pushed against the screen until it buckled. Eventually, the wire mesh fell crashing to the ground, two stories below.

He leaned out to catch his breath and hopefully spot the stupid drunk staggering round the building. The air outside tasted better than a Slurpee on a summer day. Only, it wasn't summer. And it certainly wasn't day. The landscape below had the eerie unoccupied presence of night. A chill shivered up his arms. The desolate courtyard below showed no signs of Pyen's boyfriend. He'd wished the man dead less than a full dream ago. But right now, he hoped beyond hope that he'd see the drunk stagger around the corner and pass out in the dark green grass. More than a hundred times he'd wished the man's relationship with Pyen would end, but not this way.

Unless he did.

Unless his heart prayed a true death wish.

Come on. He tipped his head back in frustration. It wouldn't be the first time his prayers for death came true. He wanted more than anything for this to be the last time. No, no, no, not the last. He wanted the last time to be the last and this time to not be one more name to add to his list.

Behind him, the fire cracked its knuckles ready to fight. The grass below beckoned him to jump. He prepared to squeeze out, but the idea of the list stopped him. Suddenly, guilt became a stronger emotion than survival. If he left without his list of the dead, he'd never have the strength to recreate it—and paper burns fast.

He looked toward the door. Smoke seeped in through the crack at the bottom, snaking to the ceiling and out the window. The list was tucked away in a shoebox under his bed. If he hurried, he'd be able to save the list and himself and then Drunk Dean. Good plan. Good plan. Good plan.

He pulled himself back into the hazy room and dropped to his knees. The junk near the bed became piles behind him as he used his hands like a dog digging a hole. A loud crash came from the front of the apartment. Frantically, he reached under his bed. His fingers crept like spiders over clothes until they found his Ute scrapbook. He pulled it out and tossed it on a pile of junk behind him.

The box would be further back. His chest hurt. The bed

frame cut into his shoulder as he reached. His fat belly wouldn't fit under the bed and the box was too far to reach, but he couldn't leave without it. Behind the door, the roaring flames knocked and an orange glow joined the flow of smoke. Small flickers licked at the top of the door. Death wasn't joking.

He turned back and focused on his rescue. This had to work. He stretched his hand further. Come on. His finger brushed against the rippled cardboard, but he couldn't get his hand around it. He pressed harder against the bed frame, but the box slipped further away.

Another loud crack.

Oh, crap.

He rolled to his knees.

Grabbing the scrapbook, he Frisbee'd it out the window.

With thick smoke swirling around his head, he tipped his bed over. The mattress landed with a thud. Awesome. He fell to his hands and knees and retrieved the box. Nothing left to do but drag the box beside him like a three-legged dog.

Back at the window, he grabbed for more oxygen and dropped the box to the ground below. He pulled his leg over the windowsill and tapped his foot on the thin ledge. He couldn't play it off—the narrow wood wouldn't hold him. But who cared? He planned to jump anyway.

Until he discovered his gut wouldn't fit through the w frame.

No way. He shook his head and squeezed his stomach as tight as possible. That gave him another inch into the two panes of glass encased in metal or plastic or whatever. The frame was impossible to budge. This couldn't be happening. He pushed until he knew if he got his stomach any further wedged in the window frame it would become a cage to hold him while he burned.

Think, Jimmy. Think. Think.

The fire's tongue lapped the ceiling and spindly orange tentacles felt their way from the tops and sides. He leaned outside and took a dozen breaths. After one last gasp, he held the air in his lungs and pulled himself back into the room. The smoke burned his eyes, but he had to find something heavy enough to break the frame.

With the curtains wide open, the streetlight illuminated all his mess in the smoky haze. There had to be something. After a second scan he noticed it. The blue bag that contained his bowling ball. That would do it.

He sucked in a couple more deep breaths from the outside and pulled himself fully into the room. With all the energy in his body, he kept the air tight in his lungs. One last obstacle and he'd be free. An interesting story to tell his counselor. He felt confident, until he forgot to get on his knees. Stupid idiot. After his first step, he tripped over junk piles and fell face-first toward the dresser. His chin caught a handle and his teeth rattled.

"Owwww!" The fresh air he'd been holding burst from his lungs. Blood replaced the taste of smoke. Great. He brought his hand to his mouth, his lips were moist from the cut. He couldn't catch a break. Much as he genuinely wanted to stop and give up, he couldn't.

Keep it moving.

Keep it moving.

Keep it moving. And no more mistakes.

He sucked the blood from his bottom lip and pressed on. In seconds, he was on the other side of his dresser. The smoke burnt his eyes, so he tapped the things around him like a blind man. The plastic handles of the bag. Yes! He wrapped his fingers around them and dragged the heavy burden back to the window. No sense removing the ball. He'd wasted too much time already. Instead, he lifted and swung the bag back and forth to gain momentum. This had to work.

In one fast arc, he tossed the entire thing toward the window. The glass of both panes shattered. The metal cracked in a glorious sound. He refused to worry about cuts or scrapes. He yanked on the frame until it broke. The happy crash of metal and glass falling to the earth thrilled him.

He climbed over the rim, glancing back into the room one last time. All edges of the door glowed, and the fire reached further into the room. His entire body now fit through the shattered frame. With one last look at the ground, he tightened whatever muscle his body had and let his fat butt fall.

CHAPTER 4

Q: *Can people buy actual dinosaur fossils?*
A: *Yes. But be careful. There are more fakes available than the real thing.*

OWWW!!

His elbow popped with pain. The hungry fire devoured the sky for more fuel. Smoke stretched up in streaks across the orange glow. The grass beneath him was morning moist. Freedom cost him more than damp pants. The stupid joint was probably busted.

Breathe.

He exhaled through his open mouth.

Breathe. Breathe. He could handle this. He could. Come on. The ache wasn't more than he'd felt a hundred times before. Heavy intakes of oxygen calmed him, and the pain. Based on the swelling, it was hopefully a sprain. Either way, he'd had enough disrupted bones to know the pain couldn't be cooled with deep breathing. Okay. What next? He had to remember. He had to focus.

The box with the list and other stuff he fought to save lay littered around him. And while fire was the most dangerous thing that paper could encounter, water was next. It would just as easily erase names from his list. The last thing he wanted to do was move, but he had to.

After plucking glass from his hand, Jimmy pulled his left arm to his chest. Searing pain returned and climbed from his elbow to his neck and up into his spine. He tipped his head back and bit his lip to fight it off. Not cool. Not cool at all. He panted until the throbbing subsided.

Just a few feet and he could stop. Just a few feet. The box lay where it landed upright, but the impact had caused the lid and a handful of things to jack-in-the-box out. Within reaching distance, the scrapbook lay open. A photo, an eagle feather and three pages from the list glowed in contrast to the lawn. The torn paper stuck to the moist grass. It was critical he recover every page. Each name was important.

Still cradling his left arm with his right, he wiped his mouth on his right shoulder. Based on the drying blood, the flow from his busted lip had slowed. Good. He swallowed. Time to move. He let go of his left arm and flipped the scrapbook closed with his right hand. Big mistake. Without the support from his right arm, the left arm screamed. He quickly tucked the scrapbook to his chest under his left arm and pinned the sprained limb with his right in an X. He swallowed back the pain and let the tears fall down his cheeks unchecked.

That was the last time he would move. He shook his head back and forth until the renewed agony ebbed away. That's it. He wasn't going to shift that sucker again.

Whew!

He breathed with his mouth opened, not caring if some jerk on a burning balcony was videotaping him for YouTube. If he looked like an idiot, he didn't care. In fact, when he allowed himself to remember he might not be alone, the sound of people yelling registered in his brain. With it came the screech of a half dozen fire alarms.

Above him, the blaze had reached into other lives. Death loved to ripple. He learned that lesson from the first time he'd killed. His own father's death rippled into over 700 names on the list. Above him, flames destroyed his room. And he would wager big money that Drunk Dean could be added to the list. Jimmy wanted to hope the man didn't die, but bigger than that he had to hope if the white man did die, he'd be the only one. He'd check the news, he was good at that. They'd tell him. The media had always been good at sharing the names of victims.

He puffed out air to dispel the worry and the pain. This stuff couldn't keep happening. It needed to stop. When his mother arrived, he would finally tell her, "Pyen, no more. Absolutely no more." In fact, if his mother brought another white man around, Jimmy would have to seriously think about leaving her to deal with it.

In the distance, sirens screamed across the neighborhood. A good sign and a bad. People would come soon. They wouldn't think twice about where they walked. The fossils and names he rescued would be trampled.

Positioned like a beggar, he sucked the smell of burnt belongings into his lungs and used his knees like feet. People in pajamas scurried from the staircase on the far side. Red and white lights flashed across the apartment walls. In the cool night air, sweat tickled the side of his face. He shook his head to get rid of it. Bad idea. His long braid slapped his mouth, renewing the pain in his upper lip. It burned and the taste of blood returned.

It was enough. The whole night was enough. For real, he wanted to stop and give up, but the sirens had arrived. The clatter of people hustled behind him. No sign of Drunk Dean, number 757 on Jimmy's list. The heaviness of the thought stopped him.

Pages lay scattered across the lawn.

An awful gurgle started in his middle. Every loose page was priceless. He had to get them before they melted into the wet earth. He couldn't pick them up with his hand. No way. He'd have to save the list another way.

Bright headlights swept over him like a prison spotlight. His crawl became hurried. The pain was manageable. For now, he couldn't let black boots on white men trample the names he rescued from the smoke-filled room. His knees hurt, but he still scrambled. Above the open box he studied the spilled items. The only way to pick them up would be with his mouth. Let's get it over with.

He bent down. The wet smell of grass mixed with the dusty taste of paper.

"Hey, stop that."

Jimmy ignored the words. He bent over to grab the page between his injured lips but couldn't quite reach when a strong arm pulled his neck up by the collar.

"Let me go."

The firefighter, a black man, took a step back. A different page crumpled beneath the man's boot.

"DON'T STEP ON MY THINGS!!"

"My bad." The man froze. "I thought you were eating the grass."

"Are you nuts?" Jimmy shook his head. He knew people thought he would stuff anything into his mouth, but this was the first time someone accused him of becoming a literal cow.

"My bad." The man said again.

"I hurt my arm." He nodded to the scattered pages around the box. "I can't use my hands."

"Let me help."

"You should help the people inside." It was stupid to hope. "My mother's boyfriend. He's—" Jimmy lifted his chin toward the window he escaped from. He sunk to his butt. Flames stretched out and up toward the third-floor window.

"I'm a paramedic. Hook and ladder are on it." The man pointed toward a couple guys attaching hoses to the fire hydrant. "We need to move away from the building." His voice was firm as he checked the ground before kneeling next to Jimmy. He kept the onlookers away while he filled the box with wet paper and photos. Finally, the black man picked up the torn page.

"You still want this?"

"Yes!"

"Man, I'm sorry."

He wanted to shrug but that would hurt his arm. Then he saw the man looking beyond him.

"You okay, son?"

Jimmy didn't have to turn around to know the new voice came from a white man. A brown man would honor him with the label "man" while whites minimized him with words like "son" or "boy." He set his jaw hard and stared at the jerk.

"Can you stand?"

"My elbow's busted up."

Eying Jimmy's whole body, the arriving paramedic sighed. "I'll get more help."

Screw him. He wouldn't be the first person to think that Jimmy was fat on accident. A lot of stupid people thought that. They didn't have brains big enough to consider someone might gain weight intentionally. Almost every quarter pound of his 269 was on purpose. Pyen said he weighed around 80 pounds when his father died.

He started the list in his seventh-grade, pre-algebra class by virtue of a mathematical discovery. If Jimmy weighed 80 pounds at seven and he subtracted that from his current weight that equaled a difference of 189 pounds. Divide that by the 756 on his list. That equals ¼ pound for each life he'd taken. A quarter-pounder for the hundreds of unintentional dead. All because an angry white man loved to beat on his half-breed boy.

CHAPTER 5

Q: *How did dinosaurs protect themselves?*
A: *Some had long tails, or spiked external skeletons, and the Ankylosaurus had huge plates of bones, like armor.*

The scrapbook lay like a sleeping baby on the ER bed beside Jimmy. The box with his list and other stuff stared at him, while the bowling ball bag mocked him. A ridiculous combination of leftovers. The only belongings he had left in life.

Above the brace on Jimmy's left elbow was a different memorial. He fingered the scar. A war wound from when his father decided to have a little fun. The beast took a jagged hunting knife and peeled back a layer of Jimmy's skin. His blood-shot eyes peeked beneath the flap as Jimmy bit back a scream.

He had just turned seven. Seven frickin' years old. And all his father could do was wipe the blade against his shirt sleeve and said, "Huh, you're not brown underneath. Guess you got my insides."

He hoped to hell not! Jimmy never wanted to be connected to any part of the white man. The arrowhead-shaped scar healed an ugly pale pink, regardless. That wasn't the first time he was abused, but it was the first time a voice inside of him rose up and shouted without making a sound, "I hope the hell not!"

He laid his right hand carefully down on the ER bed. The hospital staff had already verified the elbow sprain and put a butterfly bandage on his upper lip. None of his teeth were loose, thank goodness. They removed a few slivers of glass from his palm and dressed the wounds. The throbbing pain was subsiding even though the male nurse didn't want to give him painkillers. "Okay, James, you don't know which pain killers you're allergic to."

"Unless you want a knot on your head, don't ever call me James. Ever."

"Fine." The blonde man in bright pink scrubs didn't look mad or offended, instead he just joked. "You saved a bowling ball, but not your cell phone. You don't wear your med-alert bracelet to bed. And you don't like to be called James. Got it."

Jimmy just stared at the guy. He didn't feel like joking. This whole mess was serious to him. Deadly serious.

"No problem." The guy patted Jimmy's leg. "I called directory assistance. Your mom's boss said she's on her way."

The nurse's white shoes squeaked on the floor as he left. The antiseptic hospital smell battled with the stench of smoke from his clothes. He'd spent too many days of his life surrounded by blood and bandages. All he wanted to do was make it stop. But how could he do that? Jimmy lived in frickin' America, a land stolen from his ancestors by violent white men.

He hated his circumstances, hated that injured elbows and bruised skin were a regular part of his life, hated the violent white world. Of course, there were occasional reprieves. But honestly, the rare reprieve was worse because even a battered brain foolishly housed hope.

Sitting in the sanitized hum of the hospital, he flipped opened the scrapbook. A faded color photo of Pyen as a child stared up at him. Her mouth a straight line across her round face. She wasn't a fat child. But neither was he. To be honest, they both started getting fat after the beast died. Junk food was forbidden in that other life.

In the photo, a young Pyen stood next to two of her classmates. All three wore bear dance costumes. One smiled wide for the camera. The other one giggled behind her hand.

But Pyen stared forward with her lips in a line. A serious look of strength. If someone were to take her picture today, she'd wear the white man's mask. A smile to hide her fear. But in this picture, she looked free. Free to keep her mouth straight and her eyes off her feet.

As if summoned from his thoughts, his mother came through the door. Her body rocked back and forth as she waddled into the room. She outweighed him by at least 100 pounds. And she stood half his height. Flour clung to her black, stretch pants below where her apron had hung. Sweat stained her arms and neck. She gained her weight with Jimmy, never knowing about the list. She just followed him into fat land. He looked away, a blend of shame and anger thumped through his veins.

"Don't hug me." He stopped his mother by extending his right arm. "I hurt my elbow."

He didn't want to reject her. But the entire night had been just too heavy to carry. Forget about that. His entire life weighed more than he and his mother combined. His lower lip stung as he bit it. "Pyen, just sit down."

Her mouth went straight like in her photo. Only this time her seriousness lacked confidence. Assurance didn't show on the lips, it shone through the eyes. And Pyen kept hers toward the ground.

"I'm okay." He exhaled. "Nothing broken, just a few bruises."

She nodded and sunk into a chair beside the bed. Her eyebrows furrowed in confusion as she studied the bowling ball. A stupid thing to have in the midst of this emergency. But there it sat. The thing that saved him.

Looking back and forth from the ball and Pyen, a horrible thought emerged in his brain. There was no way his mother would have ever escaped the bedroom window. In all mathematical calculations he kept, he'd forgotten the most important one. While crippling himself under the weight of donuts and death, he'd left his mother unprotected. Besides being dangerously obese, she'd become vulnerable to the Drunk Deans of the world.

An image of his mother stuck in the window, struggling to escape the fire, tumbled from his brain to his throat in a thick lump. He swallowed. An involuntary tremble shook loose the picture of Pyen fighting her girth, unable to fit through the broken window as flames licked her back.

"You're in pain." His mother's eyes met him. "Oh my gosh. How'd this happen?"

"Are you serious?" He shook his head. "Are you actually asking that?"

She didn't look back at him. She dusted flour off her pants and changed the subject. "I told them you should not be given any NSAIDS for the pain."

He wasn't about to let her off that easy. "This isn't about today." He almost growled the next few words. "Pyen, get a clue."

She stared at him with her eyes wide.

He bit back the sudden rush of anger. He didn't want to go there. He couldn't. But, come on. "How am I supposed to know if your boyfriend started the fire and left me to burn, or if the idiot just passed out without turning off the stupid gas burner?" He exhaled. She had to know all of this. She had to. Even though he couldn't tell her that he'd wished the man dead only moments before. And that his tired request was granted. He couldn't talk to her about the list. He never could.

"Oh, Paa."

"Don't start!" He couldn't care about her concern at this moment. All the nonsense had to end. All of it. He didn't want to be a douchebag about it, but Pyen sucked at picking men and Jimmy could no longer let her bad decisions kill anyone else.

The nurse re-entered. "I've got something for your pain."

But Jimmy knew he didn't.

CHAPTER 6

Q: *Did dinosaurs eat their young?*
A: *Few animals known today actually consume their own children. When they do, it's usually to weed out large populations, or to protect itself or others.*

The big red C on the top of his Trig exam was all Pyen's fault. His home life was worthless and now that seeped into his school life. Math was easy for him. Easy as long as he didn't have to dodge drunks or escape burning buildings. He balled the paper into a fist and stuffed it in his pocket. He hadn't spoken to Pyen about the Uintah and Ouray reservation in two years. With the worst grade he'd ever had in math burning humiliation into his cheeks, he decided.

"That's it, whether she likes it or not, we're going to Utah."

"What?" A redheaded boy turned to him as Jimmy passed.

"Nothing." He didn't mean to say it aloud. He stormed to his locker. He and Pyen had to go. Not only was Drunk Dean added to the list two days ago, but three more casualties died in Afghanistan. Well, really four, but Jimmy didn't count white men. The last thing he wanted to do was add anyone else. He wanted to end it. And today, he would convince his mother to go.

With his left arm still trapped in a sling, Jimmy emptied his

27

locker using his right hand. Everything went into his backpack before he closed it with a click. The bell rang for his last class, but he didn't plan to learn one more piece of white history trivia. He'd never skipped a class before, but he'd do it today. Pyen would be waking up in ten minutes to prepare for his afternoon snack. Jimmy wanted to talk to her before she started cooking.

He walked out of Fife High School and headed toward 54th. Pyen had negotiated a cheap rate with the Quality Inn across from the casino after the owner got an exclusive with Fox news from Seattle. Another reason to get out of Dodge. The reporter promised a follow-up story.

Cars with white drivers passed him without question, but he was nervous. How many people in this area actually knew when school let out? The spring breeze tickled thin hairs across his face. On the other side of 20th Street, three or four white kids entered the swimming center as he continued to be where he wasn't supposed to. He waited for someone to grab him. A teacher. A cop. But no one did. Was it really this easy to sluff? As odd as it was to be walking around before school was out, Jimmy fought against the desire to run back to class like a good boy.

A couple more students passed him on their way toward the school. They nodded their heads at him. He caught the left-over stink of marijuana. A world he decided a long time ago he wouldn't explore. Sure, he knew kids who did it, but he refused to let anything control his functioning. Not weed. Not alcohol. Not in this life.

His palms started to sweat. The kind of PTSD sweat that joined his accelerated heartbeat. He knew he wouldn't be in trouble when he got to the motel. Pyen couldn't have found a white boyfriend in two days. Yet, the pressure in his head continued to tell him to turn around. Go back to school. Do the right thing. Stay out of trouble.

No. He shook his head. No. He continued to walk forward. No. This all had to end. He needed to get out of Washington and get to the Utah reservation. Living with members of his own tribe would fix it. It would solve everything.

He picked up a stick and started to tap it against the

sidewalk. The rhythm calmed his nerves. He didn't know much about Utah, but he knew he was Ute. Pyen didn't go into great detail, but enough to make Jimmy know that being around his own had to be better than this mess.

He crossed Pacific Highway and made it to the motel a couple minutes later ready to get away from the practically all-white world around him. The plastic keycard clicked the door open and Pyen sat on the first of two double beds.

"You're early." She looked surprised.

"Yeah." He exhaled. He wiped his hand across his forehead as if he'd run the entire distance. He went to the small fridge and pulled out a bottle of water. He didn't worry about Pyen's surprise as much as he did distraction. Once his mother started to cook, he'd never get her to focus on anything else. Another reason Jimmy knew they could move anywhere. Pyen would always find a job with her culinary skills. He tipped the bottle back and gulped down the cool water, then set the half empty plastic on the end table.

"We need to talk." He wiped his mouth on his sleeve.

"Is there a problem?"

He sat on the bed next to her. "Yeah, a big one."

"What?" The surprise in her eyes turned to panic.

"We need to get out of here."

Her eyebrows crossed together in confusion. "Is someone after you?"

"No." This wasn't coming out right. "Look, you said your cousin called after the fire to offer us a house."

"A trailer." She swallowed.

"Same difference."

"But, Paa, that's like a thousand miles away." She patted his hand. "We'll find something here. Don't worry." She started to get up but he stopped her.

"I don't want to find something here."

"Sure, you do. You have all your friends and school."

"I don't have friends." That was true. He never tried to make any. He preferred to keep people at a distance. That prevented him having to do a lot of explaining. "And I don't like school." That part wasn't true. School had been a sanctuary for him since he was four.

"What's going on?"

"I just don't want to live with white people anymore. I want to go to Utah and live on the reservation with our own people."

Her laugh started in the fat folds of her skin and tumbled out of her mouth.

He didn't like that she wasn't taking him seriously. She never did. This was their lives she was risking. "What's so funny?"

"We live on a reservation now."

"What are you talking about?" Puyallup was as white as it got. Sure, there were some native kids at his school, and Jimmy attended the native club when it didn't interfere with classwork.

"Puyallup and Fife and Tacoma, they're all on the Puyallup reservation."

"So." He didn't like the tone of her laughter. "I'm not from the Puyallup tribe anyway, I'm Ute and so are you."

She waved him away with her hand.

"Living here is not the same."

"You've got that right." Her smiled turned from humor to confirmation. "And I can promise you one thing. I'll never go back to the reservation I grew up on. Never."

"You always say that. ALWAYS!" He stood up to stand over her. "But your decisions haven't been so great, have they?"

"What are you saying?"

"I'm saying that up until now, you've hung around in the white world. Allowed it to beat you and tear you down—and I'm done with that." He slammed his fist on the table near the door and the junk food stacked there bounced from the force.

"Calm—"

"I won't calm down. I'm done calming down." He paced away from her before his impulse to smack her took over. This wasn't how this was supposed to work. She was supposed to understand. She was supposed to want to go. "I've spent my entire life having to calm down."

He turned to face her and poured all the frustration he'd ever felt into his words. "I'm done with that. And so are you. We are taking your cousin's offer and moving to Utah."

She stared at him frozen like he'd seen her stare at his father. But he didn't care. He couldn't care. This decision centered around life and death. She had to see that. She had to know it. And if she didn't right at this moment, she would.

He stormed back to her and cringed inside as she flinched. He'd never hit her. He may want to, but he never would. This was about saving their lives from that kind of violence. He grabbed her cellphone and shoved it toward her.

"Call!"

"Paa, please."

"Call," he growled. The tone matched his father's and Jimmy hated it. He should melt into an apology right now in front of the quivering mass of Jell-O that was his mother, but he couldn't. They were in danger and getting back to Utah, back to their own people, was a must.

He straightened his shoulders as his mother cowered. "Call her."

Pyen's hand shook as he kept his stance. She had no way of knowing that his heavy breathing didn't come from the same angry place as his father. It came from frustration. Desperation. Of course, she didn't know that, and his heart hurt as he continued to huff like a bull. What else was he supposed to do? He couldn't wait around for her to fall in love with another white man, bring him home so that Jimmy could kill him too.

Pyen punched the buttons.

She looked small. "Hello?" her voice trembled. "I'm calling to tell you that Jimmy and I will—" She started to cry.

Jimmy snatched the phone from her hand. She crumbled to the bed like a flattened basketball. No bounce. No life. He didn't want to feel disgusted, but that's all the emotion he could muster.

"Auntie?"

"Hi, Jimmy, what's going on?"

"Pyen told me that you have a trailer in Utah that we can live in."

"Yes, but she said she didn't want to move back here."

"Well, she changed her mind."

A miserable sob escaped from his mother. If she hadn't been

so pathetic, it might have inspired sympathy in him. But he didn't have the luxury of feeling sorry for himself or her any longer.

"Is she okay?" Pyen's cousin asked from the other end.

"Yeah, she's fine."

"Okay. This is good, Jimmy. You bring her home. I'll make sure the guy at Fairfield holds the keys for you."

"What? Aren't you going to be there?"

"No, we've moved to Montana. That's why we left the trailer. It's a good thing you called because a couple guys from the oil field showed an interest. I asked them to call me back this afternoon, but never mind that, I'd rather pass it over to family."

"Yeah, me too." Jimmy finished the conversation and had to fight back an urge to scream at his mother. He was right to skip class today. He was right to force Pyen's hand. The opportunity to move to Utah almost slipped through their hands.

He'd done it. Relief flooded through him. He exhaled.

On the bed, his mother looked up at him with an expression she'd never sent his way before. Her eyes weren't filled with the deep affection he'd know all his life. Instead, she eyed him the way she used to look at his father.

He couldn't take it. He bit his still sore lip. He'd done the right thing. He had. And doing the right thing shouldn't feel this bad. He slammed the door behind him and stormed toward a small bush beside the motel, where he vomited everything he had inside of him.

CHAPTER 7

Q: *Did dinosaurs have friends?*
A: *It is believed that some dinosaurs lived in
herds, more for protection than friendship.*

He hated himself.

He hated what it took to get Pyen to move to Vernal.

He hated that his voice had the capacity to sound like the beast's.

All of that hate drove Jimmy to change his entire outlook on death. He had to. Gaining weight was dangerous. And stupid. In the light of his new perspective, it made much more sense to sacrifice salts and sweets to those he'd killed. When he added the horrible pain of exercise to his unused muscles, he found a way to not only drop the pounds but also live with himself.

In the month it took to move to Utah, he grew stronger and felt safer. Only one worry left. How long would it take for Pyen to completely trust him again? He carried the guilt as they unpacked. As they registered him at the local high school. As he rode his bike around town.

When he couldn't take it anymore, he went ahead and Googled local cemeteries. He needed a little quiet, since the silence at home was ear-piercing. Vernal Memorial Park was only a couple of miles from the trailer park. As he pedaled along, he could only hope to recover some peace in the company of dead things. The comforting peace that comes from decaying bones.

Only three blocks into his journey he passed another potential sanctuary. A dinosaur museum with life-sized statues in its yard. He wouldn't go there today. As much as he found peace in museums, they usually contained people. The cemetery, on the other hand, would be completely empty.

Well, not completely. Void of people, yes. But not void of curiosity. Vernal had two things going for it. Not only was it near the reservation where Pyen grew up, it was also his father's hometown. Grandparents he'd never met lived somewhere close. Jimmy had no desire to meet them, but he was a little curious to see if the beast was memorialized here. His father's family hadn't come to the funeral and the military buried him on base as a hero, tri-cornered flag and all.

But did his family really fail to close that chapter of their lives? Maybe the beast wasn't worth remembering. Maybe he'd never been a gentle child. Maybe he was best forgotten. Jimmy didn't know. But this was his chance to find out, at least a little.

He pedaled up the small hill at the cemetery's entrance, ready to walk through all the graves, looking for a name. Only one problem. As he scanned the mostly level grave markers in the park, he could clearly see he wasn't alone. Seated beneath the tallest pine tree in the park, a kid who looked about ten years old huddled over a book. The afternoon sun baked Jimmy's arm as he avoided the kid and headed toward a war memorial. No way would Jimmy weave through graves under the watchful eyes of a stranger. This moment was private to him. Nobody else's business.

As Jimmy pulled up to the memorial, he could tell it was a new addition. Untattered flags snapped in the breeze. The stones lacked bird poop and wear. More and more often the cemeteries he'd visited had erected memorials thanks to Jimmy's kill skill. Everyone on his list, except Drunk Dean and boyfriend number one, were veterans.

In the center of the cemetery the kid watched him, leaving Jimmy feeling vulnerable and visible. But Jimmy could stare better than the best of them, and the two of them locked eyes. It didn't take long before the kid went back to his book. No contest at all really. Jimmy shrugged. Vernal wasn't a big city. Undoubtedly, he'd run into this kid again someday. But so what. Jimmy had reason enough to be here. Reason enough to search through the name plaques on the rectangular monument. Reason enough to be disappointed when his search provided nothing.

No James Maxwell Hunter listed on any of the engraved tags. Pyen said she'd informed the beast's family, so they knew. He didn't like how uncomfortable he suddenly felt. Pity for the beast never proved to be beneficial, even with him dead.

Suddenly he wanted to be alone more than ever. He wanted the cemetery to himself. He wanted the kid under the pine to leave. He turned his bike around. He didn't want to hurt the kid, just scare him enough to have some alone time. Another great plan until he got closer.

As the boy turned another page in what looked like a history book, Jimmy spotted a tattoo of a snake on the kid's forearm. Based on the weathered color of the ink and the way it penetrated the skin, Jimmy knew the tat was real.

He passed the kid without stopping. His urge to bother the boy had been replaced with curiosity. Not to make friends. Jimmy didn't do that. He couldn't. As he rounded the small intersection within the cemetery, a memory came back to him.

He was five years old and he'd walked home from school with a boy. The two made plans to play catch in the small backyard of base housing. Five minutes hadn't passed when the beast joined them, replacing the softball they tossed with a real baseball. Jimmy's father placed them in a triangle formation, telling Jimmy to pass to the kid, then the kid passed to the beast and the beast pelted Jimmy with the ball as hard as a grown man could. Later that day, Pyen counted thirty-three black and blue marks on Jimmy's chest, arms, thighs, and head. He avoided more than baseballs after that. He avoided friends. He never wanted another person to stare at him with pity again. And a five-year-old shouldn't have to wonder how many of the kids at school avoided him the next day because of what the boy whispered to them on the playground.

As Jimmy turned right at the next corner, drawing a circle around the kid. He didn't have to actually make friends to find out about the tattoo. He could just satisfy his curiosity as he'd done with other people in the past, then go on with his life.

He'd do it.

He'd find out.

He skidded to a stop in front of the boy and asked, "Where'd you get that?"

The kid answered without looking up. "From school."

"What kind of school gives a ten-year-old boy a tattoo?"

"I'm not ten." The boy glared up at him.

"Close enough." Jimmy shrugged then leaned over his handlebars. "Come on, tell me about the tattoo."

"Do I know you?" The boy's eyebrows came together in annoyance.

"No." Jimmy laughed. He liked that the kid didn't want to be friendly. He liked that the kid did his homework in a cemetery. And he really liked the tattoo on the ten-year-old's left forearm. "Do you have to know me to tell me about it? What is it, some kinda secret?"

"My older brother's both a jerk and a tattoo artist."

"Interesting."

The kid put his pencil in the book before closing it. "What do you want?"

"Nothing."

"Then go get it someplace else."

"You don't own this place." The desire to chase the kid away returned as quickly as it left. Jimmy suddenly wanted to really hurt the kid. He had no right to be such a jerk. Sure, Jimmy came over to chase him away, but he'd changed his mind. Now he had to force back a real desire to drop his bike and beat the kid.

"I may not own it, but at least someone I know is buried here. I doubt you can say that."

"You don't know that. I've killed enough people to fill every grave here."

"Yeah, right." The boy flipped his book back open, but Jimmy noticed the kid's hands weren't so steady.

"In fact, there's a very distinct possibility that my father should be buried here. He's from the area. Yeah. He was my first victim, but he doesn't have to be my last."

Jimmy glared.

The boy swallowed.

The snake on his arm no longer looked tough. The boy's bravado had been replaced with a wide-open stare.

Jimmy shrugged. "Don't worry, you're not worth a death prayer."

"A what?" The kid leaned forward. The sun suddenly felt hotter than anything Jimmy'd ever felt before.

"A prayer, to kill people."

"To God?"

"Or whatever." How would Jimmy know who answered his whispered requests. God. Satan. Buddha. Take your pick.

The boy's laughter started small and then grew into insults.

"This isn't funny." Jimmy's remark only tickled the boy more.

Between gasping laughs, words tumbled from the kid's mouth. "God—doesn't—kill—people." The boy pounded the ground and rolled over like a moron.

"You don't know anything." This stupid kid probably never met someone like the beast. Or Drunk Dean. Or the others. Come on. He's a white kid. White kids have the privilege of being loved by their parents. They eat mashed potatoes and meatloaf covered in gravy that always make it into their mouths, never all over their heads.

"You're actually serious." The kid sat up and wiped his eyes. "Trust me, no one can kill people with prayers." He chuckled again. "Please, if they could, the world would be incredibly underpopulated."

"You don't know crap." Jimmy glared at the jerk. "I was seven when my father was deployed to Afghanistan." Jimmy straightened his back. "I prayed for the war to last forever. Has it ended, yet?"

"You think the Afghanistan war is your fault?"

"Not the war, but its length."

"So, you're the reason for America's longest war."

37

Jimmy squinted at the sun. "I have a list of 757 people who have died because of me."

"Something's wrong with your math. Thousands have died in that war."

"I don't count the white men." Let the kid choke on that news. Every white person in the world was so sure they counted in everything. Well, not on his list. Only the men of color or women that he could find on the Internet are on my list. "No white men on my list."

"So, your dad's not white then."

"What do you know?" Jimmy kicked his pedal and let it spin. What kind of stupid assumption was that? "Of course, he's white."

"So, your dad's not on this list of yours."

"What?"

"Your white dad." The boy leaned forward. "He doesn't count, right?"

"Screw you." He'd had enough. With his tires skidding rocks at the kid, he peeled away. The jerk didn't know anything. Jimmy could put the beast and Drunk Dean and boyfriend number one on the list if he wanted. What a waste. He should have just punched the kid when he had the chance.

CHAPTER 8

Q: Were dinosaurs stupid?
A: In the 1970s scientist determined a dinosaur's
aptitude by brain size. Paleontologists in 2019 regard
dinosaurs as being very intelligent for reptiles.

Talking was pointless. He had no idea what made him open his fat trap. Since the fire, he had pretty much stopped talking to people. Well, not all people, white men to be specific. But, that scrawny kid with the annoying tattoo pissed him off so much that before he knew it, he'd spilled everything about Drunk Dean, the beast, and his list. Now he felt vulnerable and stupid. His job wasn't to pour out his history. His job was to keep himself as far away from white people as possible.

He pedaled harder as a big truck roared past him. The exhaust plumed around him in a haze. It was stupid to let his guard down. People can't be trusted. He couldn't take back the words he spilled at the cemetery, but he could make sure he kept his mouth shut the next time he saw the kid.

In fact, if he had his way, he would convince Pyen that they should go to the reservation. Vernal was close, but not close enough. Their tribal land was one place his mother refused to even talk about. On the Greyhound trip from Salt Lake City, when the bus passed the Bottle Hollow entrance, she buried her face in a magazine until they'd made it out of Roosevelt. But Jimmy couldn't give up. There had to be a way.

The wind slapped his cheeks. He leaned over the handlebars, stood on his pedals and hauled butt. The burn in his muscle relieved some of his angst.

Pyen and the reservation.

Stupid skinny white kids with tattoos.

And he'd even neglected his list. Since arriving in Utah, he hadn't really watched the news or surfed the Web for more. Losing some weight and moving to Vernal had shifted his priorities. Oh, crap. Why did life always have to be so hard?

He sunk onto the bike seat and slowed his pedaling to a dull cadence. On the other side of the world, the war still raged. Innocent men and women died. He really should go to the library and Google the fallen. But his brain was too tired to think. In fact, he still hadn't found peace, the one goal he had for the morning.

Up ahead, the dinosaur museum came into view. He exhaled. He'd love to visit a couple of old fossils if it wasn't for the tourists, but the library was a better choice. Nobody tried to talk to you there.

The last thing he needed to do was follow his desire to go straight to Wendy's. Not so long ago, eating fried or cheesy things cleared his mind, but he couldn't give in to the fat kid still lurking inside him.

He fought back the craving and listed his priorities. First, he'd appease his guilt by adding any new names to his list. Second, he'd think of a way to convince Pyen to move to the reservation. He had never lived among his own people. Indians living with Indians. He wanted to feel as much peace with the living as he did with the dead. Once he did that, the white kid problem would take care of itself. Life would be perfect.

At the museum, he slowed and pulled up to the fence. The diagonal, striped wrought iron provided a clear view of the museum yard. He wiped a sticky band of sweat from his forehead. A life-size Allosaurus model squealed in the corner. Jimmy moved toward the entrance for a better view. Through the fence he could see a two-story Diplodocus to the left of a pond where a couple baby Protoscerotops sat on rocks. Sure, most guys his age had outgrown dinosaurs, but he liked being able to look a dead beast in the eye.

The replicates were both accurate and cartoonish enough to delight. Definitely something he'd come back to see, but right now he had work to do. With a deep breath he settled into his seat, ready to leave when he noticed the old Indian standing kiddie-corner to where he sat, outside of the fence and around the corner. His wide nose and square face shouted Ute while his Levi jacket and big round belt buckle screamed cowboy.

He couldn't believe he stood within walking and talking distance to another Ute. He wanted to cry. Stupid. He was sixteen years old and not a girl. Why would his body betray him like this? But this was a real Indian. And not just any Indian. He'd met others from tribes in Washington and more than a dozen Navajo, but this man—standing close enough to touch—came from his tribe. He could actually be related to him. Not likely but the possibility made his stomach churn.

"Hey, bro." The old Indian waved at him through the fence. "Haven't seen you around here."

Jimmy couldn't talk. Instead he just shook his head and realized the action could be taken for a disagreement and nodded. Then feeling really stupid, he just said, "Hi."

"Where you from, man?"

"Washington."

"Wow." The old man lifted the brim of his mangled cowboy hat and scratched his head. "I coulda sworn you were Nuchu."

"I am." His mother told him of the Ute word for "the people" years ago. She was really good at talking about being Indian, while refusing to discuss the reservation and how to get back there. None of that mattered now, because he could ask this man everything. He turned his bike around so he could go around the corner and meet the old man. He stepped hard on his pedal only to find himself crashing to the pavement.

"Oww."

A sick scrape on his palm stung.

His shoelace was tangled in the bike chain.

He looked up. Crap. The old man was no longer visible

through the fence. Jimmy struggled to his feet and attempted to hop-drag the bike around the corner without massacring his nuts in the process. It took forever, given the height of the bar in the middle of the bike. By the time he rounded the corner, the old man was gone.

CHAPTER 9

Q: *Did dinosaurs make nests?*
A: *Yes, some dinosaurs returned to
the same nesting site every year.*

Jimmy hustled a couple times around the museum.

The man had evaporated. Crazy. Maybe the old Indian wandered into the museum. Jimmy dumped his bike and went inside. Beyond the doors, in the center of the wide-open room he stood stunned at what he saw. His heart accelerated in his chest.

Looming before him, an amazing skeleton took up the height and breadth of the room. By its long neck and tail, he knew this would be one of the large herbivores. Maybe a Diplodocus. He stepped forward. The beast surpassed the massive models in the yard. Jimmy exhaled. This was why he loved the dead. They were grand and amazing and touchable. They made museums and graveyards their home. Quiet places with no screaming or hitting or hate, just the soft quiet of things who couldn't hurt or be hurt ever again. Including the monster before him.

"Excuse me." The comment killed his joy and broke the spell. An older, white woman stood behind a counter dressed in a tan uniform. "Can I help you?"

"No."

He approached the large dinosaur. No glass or gates or bars separated him from the massive skeleton. He touched the leg bones, black like stone. The beast was large enough that he could actually duck beneath the massive ribcage.

"Son?"

He clenched his fists and pivoted on his heels. "I'm not your son, and I don't need help."

"Maybe not." She glared at him. "But, to come in here, you need to pay."

He swallowed.

He didn't have any money on him. He was too new to Vernal to have found a job. He wiggled his fingers as he released them. "Oh . . . umm. Well, I'm looking for a friend." He hated more than anything to look stupid in front of white people.

"You still have to pay." The scowl remained stolid on her face.

He pushed back his frustration and approached the desk. "My friend would have come in right before me. An old man, Ute like me."

"I can save you some time and money." She didn't have to sound so happy. Didn't have to but did. "No one has entered in the last fifteen minutes."

His fingers curled into the palm of his hand. He took one last look over his shoulder at the large skeleton. On another day, he be back with plenty of money to shove at the grumpy guard. Outside, he circled the museum one last time and decided to head into town. The old man must have gone in that direction or Jimmy would have passed him when he freed his shoelace from the bike gears. He pumped his way past the Vernal Police Station, hoping the old man had no business there.

After a couple more blocks, Jimmy knew he'd have to keep track of each turn. Google told him the best route from the trailer park to the cemetery. Looking behind him, he noted the straight line from here to the museum. He pedaled past another street, another detour the old man could have taken. Squinting didn't help. By the time he reached Vernal Avenue, he fought back his pride and decided to ask someone.

Besides the passing trucks coughing out smelly exhaust, the only person he could see was a white man in a John Deere baseball cap. The disheveled man leaned against the brick wall of a building. The nerves in Jimmy's gut twitched.

He'd been silent with every white man over sixteen since he left the hospital, not saying a single word to even his teachers. The most he'd given was a nod. Should he break that now? That stupid white kid at the cemetery made him feel like a regular chatterbox. But if he wanted to make friends with the only Indian he'd seen since he arrived, something had to give. The reservation was near. His horrible childhood could end in a couple dozen miles. The impossible dream of finishing high school in a place where he was part of the majority.

That dream was enough to push past his silence and ask, "Have you seen an old Indian walking down this way?"

"You mean Coyote Joe." The man switched his chew from his left cheek to the right and spit a wad into the gutter near Jimmy's bike tire. The stink of sweat surrounded the jerk. "Yeah, he passed by here."

"Which way?" After asking, Jimmy held his breath to keep from breathing in the stench of this jerk.

"The way he always goes." The man tipped his head in the direction Jimmy was already heading. "Check the dumpsters."

"The what?" His fingers curled around the handlebars on his bike. There were days when he wished he could find a single white man who didn't have something bad to say about Indians. "Is that some kind of joke?" He crossed his arms knowing the action made his biceps thicker.

"Cool your britches." The man pulled off the wall. When the idiot got to his full height, he was three to four inches taller. "Go see for yourself." He looked down his nose at Jimmy before hawking another wad onto the sidewalk at Jimmy's feet. With a sarcastic smile on his lips, he touched his fingers to the brim of his hat and walked away.

Life offered two choices in moments like this. Fight or flight. Most guys believe flight evokes cowardice. Jimmy knew better. That jerk could try to climb into his brain and distract him from his goal, but he refused to yield his power. He had walked away from a lot better reasons to punch someone.

Didn't mean he didn't want to but wanting and doing should always be calculated. Instead, he let out the breath he'd been holding and made his way to the back of the stores. He already hated Vernal. The insane ratio of white to brown faces. The harsh expression on those faces. People in this town were overly hostile. After humiliating himself by looking into or behind about thirty trash containers, he accepted that he wouldn't find Coyote Joe today. He went home, ready to do the same stinky disgusting thing tomorrow and the next day until he found the man.

CHAPTER 10

Q: *What did dinosaurs use as camouflage?*
A: *Dinosaurs, like many of today's reptiles, probably had skin that could hide them in plain sight.*

Coyote Joe was like a ghost to Jimmy after his initial sighting. Vernal had become a horror movie where he was forced to search shadows. What would it take to talk to this guy? Life didn't have to be this hard, throwing crap in Jimmy's way.

One day he'd seen the old man pass by in the back of a truck with a sign that read Mother's Funeral. On another day he stood on the opposite side of Highway 40, the busy section near Wendy's, Arby's and Little Caesars' "Pizza Pizza." Jimmy didn't have his bike and the old man slipped away before the endless traffic died.

Coyote Joe appeared twice while Jimmy was with Pyen. The first time they were outside of Davis Jubilee. Pyen didn't make eye contact, but Jimmy did. He smiled and nodded but couldn't have the conversation he wanted. The food stamps in his mother's purse humiliated him too much.

"Stay away from that vagrant," she said once they passed through the sliding glass doors.

He didn't answer. No sense in lying to her about it. Not when she didn't insist, he answer. No, he'd wait for another

47

time. He had to. Nothing would stop him from connecting with Coyote Joe.

And as if the universe knew Jimmy was serious, less than a week later, the old Indian slump past the high school on a morning Pyen and he had a meeting with the school counselor. This was his chance. And his best means of escape would be to pick a fight with her.

"Pyen." He made his tone hard. "I hate this school."

"Why?" She parked the old beat-up Malibu she'd bought off Craigslist last week.

"I want to live on the reservation. Go to school with my own people."

"These are your people." She scowled.

"No, they're not."

He waited for her to pry her way out of the car. She didn't look at him. "Paa, this is the school you're going to."

"That's not fair."

"Knock it off."

He stopped outside the front doors. "I'm old enough to decide."

"Jimmy." Her voice tightened.

He glared at a student who hurried past them. "I hate these white people. I have a right to live on the reservation."

"No." She held the door open.

"Why not?" He said it hard. He made sure his expression was both loud and angry.

"Because."

"Not good enough. Tell me, NOW!"

She didn't say anything. Instead she went inside and allowed the door to close behind her. He didn't follow. As far as she knew, he was upset. Good, that meant she wouldn't follow him. Instead, she'd have the consultation without him.

Across the grass, Coyote Joe still clomped. Jimmy dashed toward him, elated the old man hadn't disappeared on him again. He felt like he'd found a hundred-dollar bill on the ground, but this was better than money. Under a blue sky, in the moderate heat of spring in the desert, Jimmy was about to talk to the one guy who could rescue him from a life with whites.

"Hey, there," Jimmy shouted. He fought back the desire to pat the man on the back as he approached. They weren't old friends. Yet.

"Oh, hey." Coyote Joe's hand trembled as he removed it from his coat. "Yeah, hey."

"I ran over from the school to meet you."

The old man didn't look surprised. He just fumbled a little with his hat and kept walking. Maybe he had a vision of Jimmy coming, an intuition. Indians could feel things before they happened. "Are you skipping classes?"

"No, my teachers want to talk to my mom. I don't need to be there."

Coyote Joe stuffed his hands back into his pockets and continued to the stoplight. They cut across the traffic-free intersection at a diagonal. "Don't drop out, man."

"I won't." He smiled. Those four words from this man meant something. A word of concern. They felt full of protection and peace, the kind he'd find among his own people. Jimmy hadn't been wrong about wanting to meet this man. He could feel his heart swell. "Can I ask you a question?"

"Sure."

"How far is the reservation from here?"

"That depends on who you talk to, man." Coyote Joe kicked a rock with the toe of his old cowboy boot. "Far as I'm concerned, you're standing in it now."

"I thought the entrance was down the highway."

"Sure, the allotment's over there, but all of this land was open to Nuchu before the white man arrived."

Jimmy smiled. He knew these things. He knew how the white world put up fences and wrote their own laws to steal what they could from the Indians. But this was the first time he could talk openly about those injustices. This was his chance to escape all that. "How can I get to the part of our land still run by Indians?"

"That part?"

"Yeah."

The old man lifted a single-shoulder shrug. "Depends. If you want to go down the highway to Bottle Hollow, it's easy to get in." They crossed the open grass past the baseball diamonds. "But you sound like you want to go and stay."

"I do." His heart felt light at the words. Free. "I want to live there."

"Well. That's not so easy."

"Why not?"

"Politics. Tribal elders. You name it." Coyote Joe lifted his hand and waved at a couple of guys sitting under the pavilion. "Listen, man, you go on back to school. I've gotta talk to my friends over there."

Jimmy stopped. The man was busy, of course. Jimmy understood that, but that didn't stop the heaviness of disappointment to crash onto him.

Coyote Joe kept walking. "Don't worry. We'll talk about the rez later, man." His steps quickened as he passed the clutter of bright colored slides and climbing bars. Jimmy sat on one of the empty swings, remembering a time when it was uncomfortable squeezing into them. He kicked at the woodchips feeling a mix of hope and disappointment. The rez. Cool. The dismissal, not so much.

Over his shoulder, the men in the pavilion huddled around the old man when he arrived, including some idiot with a John Deere hat. Jimmy didn't want to feel the hovering sense of abandonment that haunted him like death, so he pushed it down. Coyote Joe said they'd meet again, all Jimmy could do was trust him. He headed back toward the school doing everything he could to forget about how happy the old man looked clowning it up in the circle of white men.

CHAPTER 11

Q: *What did dinosaurs eat?*
A: *Most dinosaurs were plant eaters. Only a few were considered carnivores, or meat-eaters.*

Six days later, Jimmy sat in class unsettled and unsatisfied. The whiteboard contained the water cycle. His science teacher was talking about complex weather patterns, specifically virga, a phenomenon unique to desert regions. The thick clouds that tease the earth with the promise of rain that was as elusive as Coyote Joe.

Jimmy would never make it to the reservation at this pace. He had to find a faster way. Freedom was too close. Besides, if the old Indian was right, everyone in Vernal lived on the reservation. That means anyone who lived here would know about it. Right?

He looked around the classroom. How many of these kids could help him? The only one he might approach was the know-it-all from the cemetery. Yeah, turned out the boy with the snake tattoo wasn't ten years old after all. He was in Jimmy's math and science classes.

He hadn't spoken to him since that first day, but he felt the kid was his best shot at finding some information. Best shot because at least they'd already met. Already spoken. Without the pressure of having to start from scratch.

Once he made up his mind to go for it, he found it almost as difficult as talking to Coyote Joe. First, he tried to say something after the bell, but a couple other boys were with the kid. Next, he almost sat with him at lunch, until two girls from the choir asked the kid to move. Jimmy would have sat with the boy, if the kid had chosen another seat, but instead the boy just dumped his tray and left the room. It would have been too obvious to follow him. Too sketchy, so he sat at a table in the corner and ate.

After two more failed attempts Jimmy had pretty much decided he'd try again tomorrow. He headed to the bike racks. Most high schoolers drove or took the bus, only a handful, like Jimmy, came on bikes. But the weather was sweet and three other bikes were locked on the metal rails. And to Jimmy's surprise, one of them belonged to the kid. The idea of chatting with the boy had been one-hundred percent right. This was proof.

Jimmy watched from behind the glass door as the boy unlocked his bike. Once he got situated and pedaled away, Jimmy stepped outside and saw the kid head for the tunnel under 500 North.

This was perfect. It would be way easier to talk to the boy off school property and away from the harsh judgments of the other students. It was fate! What were the chances that they both had bikes? A significant sign. Jimmy still had no idea exactly what he'd say or how he'd start the conversation. Distracted at the thought, he actually messed up the combination on his bike lock twice. Come on. This stupid bike always choked in the clutch.

Seven.

Twist left.

Fourteen.

Twist right back to one.

Click. Yes! Finally. He pulled out the chain and stuffed it into his backpack. He could only hope the kid hadn't disappeared. Vernal had become a place where Jimmy spent more time looking than finding. A very different life than the one he knew before. Crunches instead of couch surfing. Stalking people like Coyote Joe and this kid instead of checking the Internet for the names of the dead. His legs hurt from working out, but he was surprisingly a lot less tired these days.

He quickly checked the chain before climbing onto the seat. He looked over at where the kid might have gone and quickly spotted him about a block and a half down, heading toward the park. The same path Coyote Joe took a few days ago. Instead of using the tunnel, Jimmy cut across the grass toward the Seminary building.

He thought he'd catch the boy at the light, but the kid was pretty fast. Jimmy turned on the paved surface between the baseball diamonds, shortening the distance to less than a block away. He stood on his pedals and tried his best to catch up. It took another two blocks and Jimmy was winded. The boy finally waited at the stop sign near the car wash. It was a four-way stop, but the boy just stayed there staring at a guy spraying off his truck.

"Hey, graveyard," Jimmy said pulling up next to the kid.

"What?" The kid looked annoyed before checking for traffic and crossing the street.

Jimmy followed. "You don't have to cop an attitude, I just wanted to say hello."

"So?"

"Does everyone in Vernal have a stick up their butts?"

"Yeah, what of it."

"Never mind." Jimmy's bright idea turned stupid in an instant.

His heart sank.

Why now? He shook his head as he watched Coyote Joe pop up and down in the dumpster like a Muppet.

At the Taco Bell he pulled into the parking lot and let tattoo boy continue toward the light. But even though they were on different trajectories, Jimmy realized they both could see the same thing.

"Hey," Jimmy scolded the old man as he pulled his bike up next to the bin. He felt humiliated for the old man. He'd spent the last month fighting back fast food cravings, but he couldn't imagine ever being desperate enough to dig in the trash.

"Get out of there." He squinted up at Coyote Joe.

"I'm hungry, man."

The horrible smell of rotting fast food made Jimmy kick the dumpster. Unfair. Jimmy had consumed millions of calories from clean plates while one of his own people scraped a meal from the trash. "Get out, I'll feed you."

"Really?" The man's wrinkled face brightened. "Awesome."

As Coyote Joe struggled to escape the bin, Jimmy caught the boy staring at them both from the sidewalk opposite the drive thru. He hadn't ridden away, instead he'd stopped to watch the entire show. "What are you staring at?"

"Nothing." The boy should have left. He should have sped away and left Jimmy to deal with the old Indian by himself.

Instead, Coyote Joe chimed in, "Don't chase your friend away. The two of you can help me out of here."

"He's not my friend."

"Sure, he is," the old man said. "Everyone's your friend if you let them."

Jimmy didn't want to argue with the old man. Especially since it was so hard to find him. He had zero desire to share Coyote Joe with the boy, but he couldn't risk looking cruel either. Fine. "Hey, graveyard, stop staring like a dweeb and help out."

"You shouldn't talk to people like that."

"Me?" Jimmy couldn't believe it.

"Yeah," the kid crossed the grass to help. "You got a stick up your butt or something?"

Coyote Joe laughed and Jimmy seethed. This white kid just wanted to embarrass him in front of the old Indian. Problem was, it was working. Jimmy glared at the kid as the old man asked the boy for his name.

"Devin."

"I'm Coyote Joe." The old man handed the boy his bag and gave Jimmy a thick walking stick. Jimmy resisted the urge to smack Devin with it and instead focused on getting Coyote Joe out of the dumpster. It was a struggle. After a few elbows in the face, the old man landed hard on his feet and adjusted his Levi jacket. The food Coyote Joe stuffed in his pocket didn't reek. He dusted off his clothes and said, "Nice to meet you boys."

"We met before." Jimmy didn't want to feel hurt the old Indian didn't remember him. Stupid. They hadn't talked long. And he was an old man. The irritation he felt had to be connected to the proximity of Burrito Supremes.

"Oh, right. Yeah. Hi, kid." But the man's eyes lacked recognition. Kindness, but no acknowledgement. None of this was going the way he imagined. Maybe once he got the old man home and fed, he could focus his mind on the rez. "Come on, I live over in Fairview Trailer Park."

"Is that a good idea?" Devin leaned toward Jimmy.

Jimmy rolled his eyes. "You don't have to come if you don't want."

"No." The boy shrugged. "I'm good."

"Fine," he pointed his bike back toward Highway 40. "Let's go."

"But Fairview Trailer Park is this way." The kid pointed down the side street. "My school bus passes it every day."

He looked over his shoulder. He didn't like people bossing him, especially not in front of Coyote Joe. He agreed, but only because he hadn't mastered his way around Vernal.

"Then lead." He thrust his hand toward the so-called better way.

Devin rolled his bike down the narrow sidewalk. Coyote Joe stomped behind him and Jimmy made the tail.

Above them wanna-be rain clouds hovered. He called them wanna-be because they promised rain without delivering it. Gray clouds hung on the horizon with rain streams stretching toward the desert earth. The water never reached the ground. It dried up before it reached the tallest trees. The pointlessness of it reminded Jimmy that it would be easier if he could cherish the peace at home. The lack of violence. Settle into life with Pyen until he graduated. But a desire for permanent peace nagged at him.

If he ever wanted to be truly free, he'd have to get to the reservation. But first he'd have to get Coyote Joe away from the kid without looking like a jerk.

CHAPTER 12

Q: *Did dinosaurs have parasites?*
A: *The University of Colorado at Boulder found a preserved dinosaur fossil with apparent wormholes in its gut.*

It wasn't the walk that tired him. It wasn't the occasional truck that puffed out fumes at them along the way. It wasn't even the endless sea of white faces that made all the energy drain from Jimmy's limbs. No. Instead, on the corner of Vernal Avenue and 500 North, Coyote Joe invited Devin to go to the reservation.

Jimmy's heart hurt. No frickin' way. This was his day. His moment. He tried to squeeze between the two of them, but the traffic cleared at the busy intersection and the three had to take their opportunity to race across.

Devin took the lead while Jimmy rolled his bike behind Coyote Joe.

Safely on the other side, the old man caught up with the white boy. "Yeah, man, I've got a ride to the rez on July 3rd for powwow. It's in the back of a pickup—long as you don't mind a little wind in your hair."

Devin didn't answer. Jerk. The white boy wasn't going to go to the reservation and hang out with a bunch of screaming Indians. White boys didn't go for that kind of untamed emotion.

Not that Jimmy had ever been to a real powwow, but he'd seen a few on YouTube. It was an all-native affair. No white people allowed.

"I'd love to go. In fact–" Jimmy walked his bike into Fairview Trailer Park "–I'd like to go even sooner. July's more than a month away."

Coyote Joe shrugged. "I don't know, man."

Jimmy didn't press it. They'd have time during lunch to talk. First, he needed to get rid of Devin. "Okay, we're close enough, you can go home now."

"Maybe he's hungry too," Coyote Joe said as he scuffed his hand across Devin's cropped hair cut. The boy pulled away, but it was hard to tell if he was disgusted or just didn't like his hair touched. Unbelievable, the two had somehow bonded.

"Yeah, sure." Jimmy felt suddenly lost. He wanted Coyote Joe all to himself, but the old man seemed to prefer the company of the white boy. For now, he had to let the kid stay, at least until he could get the man's address or phone number or even the name of someone else who could help him. "As long as we talk more about the reservation."

"You bet, man." Coyote Joe surveyed the neighborhood. "Are we close?"

"Just past that stop sign." Jimmy nodded.

"Cool."

The old man pressed on while Devin grabbed Jimmy's sleeve.

"You can't go to the powwow with that guy!" the white boy whispered.

"Watch me."

"You don't even know him," Devin hissed.

Jimmy shook him off. "Why don't you just go home?"

They turned into Fairview Trailer Park. "Nice digs, man." Coyote Joe nodded.

"Thanks." Jimmy hated the place. It didn't matter how many times he entered the trailer park, he always wanted to blow it to bits. Gravel driveways. Rusted trailers with cinder block steps. He watched for Devin's reaction only to find the kid was too busy watching Coyote Joe to notice anything else.

"So," the boy didn't whisper now. "When you're at the powwow, where will you stay?"

Jimmy dropped his bike near the base of the singlewide. "What are you, my dad all of a sudden?"

"No."

Jimmy unlocked the door. "Then stop butting in where you're not wanted."

"No, man, it's cool." Coyote Joe almost sung the words. "The kid can come too. We can all camp with my buddies."

Ha. Perfect. Jimmy didn't need to make Devin look bad in front of the old man, the white boy would do it all by himself. "Yeah, Devin, want to come hang out with the Indians. Stay in a teepee?"

Coyote Joe shook his head. "No, man. My friends and I don't put up teepees. Too much work."

Jimmy bit his lip. He didn't mean a real teepee. Oh, crap. Now he sounded stupid. Forget it. It was best to pretend the idiotic white boy wasn't there. This was the rare chance to pick Coyote Joe's brain and he wasn't about to let some dumb kid mess it up. He pushed open the aluminum door and entered the trailer. Coyote Joe and Devin followed close behind.

The scent of Pyen's lavender candle mixed with the odor of Old Spice. He sniffed again in reflex, like a drug-smelling police dog. Faint but there. The same nasty stuff that the beast used to wear. His knees suddenly felt weak, and not from the long walk to the trailer park. The scent must be from the kid or the old man. It had to be. The only reason he didn't smell it before was because they were outside. There was no way Pyen had a boyfriend.

"Got any cookies?" Coyote Joe plopped down on the worn sofa.

"Sure."

Jimmy shook off the sense of dread. They'd been in Vernal less than a month. Definitely not enough time for Pyen to find a man. He headed to the pantry, fighting back his concerns. From a top cupboard, he grabbed an unopened package of Oreos. The old Indian took the entire pack. He opened them but didn't offer one to Devin. Instead he just said to the kid.

"Nice tat."

"Thanks." The white boy covered the ink with his hand.

"But snakes bring bad mojo, man."

"Thanks." This time Devin let a little sarcasm seep out.

Jimmy didn't join in the conversation. He was too busy pushing away thoughts of his mother and an impossible new boyfriend. The smell of chocolate cookies with cream filling had already replaced the awful scent of cologne. Better to focus his attention on feeding the old guy without messing with his routine. He needed to make something hearty for the hungry man, but nothing he'd be tempted to eat.

The waft of cool air from the refrigerator helped. He'd let Pyen own the cupboards as long as she promised not to put anything fattening in the fridge. He stared at the two heads of lettuce, knowing Coyote Joe would probably leave if Jimmy offered him a salad. Instead he pulled open the bin that contained packets of processed meats—something he found strangely satisfying while also low in calories, as long as he stayed away from mayonnaise and bread.

Hot dogs.

Perfect.

Jimmy pulled out the package and dropped it on the table. Pyen loved canned pasta which matched perfectly with questionable meat. He would eat a hot dog while the old man could have the full carb lunch. Good. Jimmy felt satisfied. The underlying worry of a new man in Pyen's life subsided. That was crazy thinking anyway. He turned his attention back to his guests.

"Is the powwow the only time visitors can go to the reservation?"

Devin laughed. "You make it sound like an amusement park."

Coyote Joe laughed too.

"What do you know?" Jimmy pointed the can opener toward the obnoxious kid.

"More than you, obviously."

"So, you think people can just wander over there without an invitation." Jimmy slammed a large can of SpaghettiOs onto the counter. "You think just because you're white you can just go around wherever you want, whenever you want."

"Um, yeah." The boy shrugged. "It's not a zoo."

No, he didn't. Jimmy slammed the can opener onto the counter. "Are you calling Indians animals?"

"No, I think you are. The reservation is a neighborhood that happens to be on sovereign land. You're the one who seems to think it should be off limits to people."

"No, I don't."

"I think you do."

"It's okay," Coyote Joe held up his hands. "It's not worth arguing about." His teeth were black with cookie dust. "Let's just get along, man. I don't like fighting." He shoved another cookie in his mouth.

Jimmy exhaled. Fine. He glared at the white boy before turning his back on both of them. This afternoon couldn't be more messed up. He should never have tried to talk to the stupid white boy. Noodles and red sauce slopped from the large can into the big bowl. He wanted to hear more about the powwow and drum circles and freedom. The thought of being with his own people pulled at the corners of his mouth. Indians with Indians, no whites allowed. But the stupid boy made it sound like Jimmy was the racist.

"Do you have a bathroom?" The old man stood up.

"Yeah. Down there." He pointed toward the first door in the small hallway.

Coyote Joe clomped down the hall. Jimmy shoved the bowl into the microwave and set the timer to two minutes. Devin got up and walked over to the table. "Look, you don't have to be a jerk to me. I'm just trying to help you here."

"Help me?"

"Yes, that old guy's trouble, I tell you."

"Who asked you?"

"You invited me. And you don't know that dude."

"And you do, mister know-it-all?"

"Yes. You don't know who you're messing with. That homeless guy is nuts. Half the town walks on the other side of the street to avoid him. He has a knife in that bag big enough to cut even your fat head off with."

"That's racist." Jimmy stared him down, but the boy didn't flinch.

"Don't you have that twisted?"

"No." The sound of shifting gravel stopped Jimmy from telling the boy off. "Oh, crap." He pushed away from the counter.

"I'm serious." The boy followed him.

"I'm not talking to you."

He had bigger problems than Devin right now. Through the small kitchen window, he'd seen his mother's Malibu pull under a tree. She was going to freak finding Coyote Joe in her house. "My mom's coming." He grabbed the bag of hot dogs and headed down the hall. She'll ruin everything.

He pounded on the bathroom door. "I've got to get you out of here, my mom's coming."

Jimmy heard the old man curse through the thin door. He turned to his bedroom across the hall and set the hot dogs on the bed.

"Whadya want me to do?" Devin stood at his shoulder.

"Keep my mother busy while I sneak him out." He hoped the old man would fit through the bedroom window. The glass slid up with a loud creak. The old man came out of the bathroom as fast as an arthritic hound.

"Come on." Jimmy pulled him in and closed the bedroom door. He leaned against it and heard his mother call for him, "Paa?"

"Be out in a minute," he hollered, then pressed his ear tight against the door.

He had zero reason to trust Devin. The white boy had been nothing but trouble all day. Yet at this moment the boy was the only one left to trust. The last thing he needed was to be grounded and lose the one avenue he'd found to the reservation.

"Are these for me?" Coyote Joe still had the Oreo's hugged to his chest and grabbed the bag of hot dogs before he could answer.

"Shhh." He put a finger to his mouth and waited until

Coyote Joe saw the gesture and nodded.

"Sorry, man," Coyote Joe whispered.

With his ear to the door, Jimmy heard Devin tell his mother he went to the bathroom. He exhaled. The boy covered for him as Pyen became more interested with what was in the microwave. The boy lied for him, which meant more to Jimmy than his heart could hold. He couldn't think of a moment in his life when someone covered for him. Sixteen years of fighting against white men had been very isolating. He couldn't dwell on that now. Coyote Joe needed an escape route.

At the window, the screen popped out and fell into the tall grass. He hated to send the old man through the window. It wasn't right. "I'm sorry."

"No problem, man." Coyote Joe slipped from the house like a pro. "Thanks for the food."

Jimmy fought back the strong instinct to join the old man. "Where can I find you?" He asked in hushed tones.

"Anywhere the moon is full and the grass is green and the ladies are sweet." The old man handed the screen up to Jimmy who fitted it back in place.

As Jimmy slid the window back down, disappointment filled him. Coyote Joe navigated his way around the back of the other trailers, lifting the cookies and hot dogs above his head as a sign of thanks.

Jimmy let the disappointment hang on him. Only one thing left to do. Get back into the living room and tell Pyen he wanted to take Devin home. They could still catch the old man.

He hurried into the kitchen. Pyen wasn't mad about finding Devin in the house. She was too excited telling the white boy all about her new boyfriend.

CHAPTER 13

Q: *How did dinosaurs get so big?*
A: *Unlike mammals, reptiles continue to grow their entire lives. The oldest crocodile on earth will be the biggest.*

Jimmy kicked the back tire on the Malibu. The human mind could only deal with so many problems at one time. He kicked the tire again. The stupid car blocked his bike, his exit, his life. He fought back the urge to take his fist and pound the trunk again and again. Instead he picked up a rock and chucked it into the field as hard as he could.

"Are you okay?" Devin sat on his bike, staring at him with an open jaw.

"I don't want to talk about it."

He yanked his bike from the front of the car, scratching it against the bumper. "Stupid car."

He climbed on and rode away from the house. His mother said they could go outside and play. Crap, she still thought he was a baby or something.

"Jimmy, wait!"

The white boy screamed, but he stood on his pedals and sped onto 500 North, ready to escape them all when a loud horn blasted. He tumbled to the shoulder. The skid of truck tires accompanied the burnt smell of brakes as he landed hard in the tall grass.

"Watch where you're going!" the jerk shouted before speeding off down the supposed-to-be twenty-five-mile-per-hour road.

"Get in line!" Jimmy screamed back.

He kicked his bike without getting up. This town had too many stupid trucks. Too many frickin' white people. Too many disappointments. He let his head fall into his hands as Devin plopped down beside him.

The fifteen-minute conversation that had happened after Coyote Joe left had his head spinning. He'd felt so much hope when he and Pyen first arrived in Vernal. Being close to the reservation blinded him to the reality of Pyen's habit. "A boyfriend. Is she nuts?"

"What's the big deal?" Devin pulled at a yellow stalk of grass.

"Boyfriends are dangerous." He pounded his hand against his knee. "Oh, crap." People never understood. Unless you have immediate bruises or broken bones, control and abuse aren't seen. Maybe not even believed.

"Oh . . ." The white boy nodded the way Jimmy'd seen him do in class. "Your list."

He glared at the kid. "Yes. The list. Look, I know you don't believe me. But trust me when I tell you, my mother doesn't need a boyfriend. I told you about the list, but what I didn't tell you is why we moved to Vernal."

The boy waited.

Jimmy waited too. He didn't honestly know if he should tell this boy anything. He was so confused. First Coyote Joe was too frickin' elusive and Pyen, well forget about her. He grabbed three stalks of grass and started to braid it. Jimmy didn't have anyone he could talk to.

"What made you move?"

"A fire." The weaving helped. It calmed him. Might as well spill it to this kid. Might as well tell the world. "My mother's last boyfriend decided to leave bacon grease burning on a gas stove top before he passed out drunk."

"No way."

"Yes, way. That's why the last thing my mother needs is a boyfriend."

"This one could be different."

"No." He grabbed three more stalks of grass and started to braid it. "It's never different. Never."

Devin stared at his fingers as Jimmy wove the stalks of grass together, alternating one over the other and adding more as he got close to the end. A skill he learned from his mother. In fact, it often helped in PTSD moments as well.

"What are you doing?"

"Weaving, dummy."

"You don't have to call me names."

He didn't, but this was one of those moments when everything he believed was tied tight began to unravel. In fifteen short minutes, the world became unsafe again, like leaving a dark theater after an intense action movie and finding himself scanning the neighborhood for armed enemies. "Sorry, I didn't mean it, but I've got bigger problems on my hands."

"Your mom made him sound nice."

"She would." Jimmy tightened the band before adding a new blade to the rope.

"He's taking you to the quarry. That's cool."

What a dweeb. "This is not about the quarry. This is about the man."

"But he's a sheriff's deputy."

"And?"

"Well." The kid shrugged. "I don't think they are allowed to get drunk and burn stuff up."

"Are you kidding?" Devin couldn't know—he was born white in an all-white world. He'd never know the complex layers of discrimination. "The last thing Pyen and I need is another white man hanging around."

"But how do you know her new boyfriend is white?"

Was he nuts? "Have you been to Vernal, Utah?"

"Very funny."

"Please, this place is as white as it comes."

"Except the reservation." Devin said.

"Except the reservation," Jimmy repeated.

That's right. He took in a deep breath. The burnt scent of rubber lingered, but he could make out the smell of dry grass and hope. The rez. The answer to all his problems. Crap, if he could live on the rez, he probably could save Pyen and even give up list making and everything. He dropped the band he'd woven.

The thought of not keeping the list made him nervous. It had been an important part of his life for so long, a way to process the abuse, the deaths. The desert sun baked his bare arms. He couldn't think about losing that list now. Instead, he needed to find Coyote Joe and go to the reservation. Of course, that would be hard without help.

Devin picked up and studied the braided strand on both sides. Jimmy had a choice. Trust this boy or rescue his mother alone. When his dad lived, he survived. When boyfriend number one plowed his car into a tree, he hunkered down. When Drunk Dean burned to death, he escaped. All of this without anyone else's help. Independence had been fundamentally safer in his experience than companionship. Yet, here they sat.

The kid hadn't ratted him out when his mother came home or run from the dumpster earlier. He hadn't even acted shocked with his history, only interested.

"Why did you lie to my mom back there?"

"I didn't lie."

"Yes, you did. You told her I was in the bathroom."

"No." He shook his head adamantly. "I said you went to the bathroom. Which—" he lifted his finger "—you did."

Jimmy laughed. This kid was great. Determination, not happiness, caused a smile to climb over his face. ""Come on, we need to find Coyote Joe."

"Again?" Devin groaned.

"Yes." He took out his cell phone. "What's your number?"

With a confused look, Devin gave the digits still clutching the grass band.

"I'll make you one of these if we find him." He lifted the leg of his pants and showed him a woven friendship band tied around his ankle.

"Cool." Devin nodded.

He dialed Devin's number and heard the standard ring tone coming from the kid's backpack. "That's my number. Look, I'm heading to the park. You check the museum. If you find him call me." Jimmy got up and hurried away, certain the white boy would help. Coyote Joe had to be found. And fast!

CHAPTER 14

Q: *Did dinosaurs watch over their young?*
A: *Nest evidence has suggested baby dinosaurs were possibly fed and protected by their parents.*

Jimmy searched for Coyote Joe until the sun set. Devin said he did too. The city was against them. The town full of exhaust-coughing trucks refused to give up the old man. Day after day, their search only led to one more crossed-off date on the calendar, Uintah High held their graduation on Friday.

Jimmy wasn't going. He didn't know any seniors. Obviously neither did Pyen's new boyfriend, because today was when the devil had chosen to hold their stupid visit to the dinosaur quarry. Of course, the man was white and white men ruined everything. Between their violent need for control and their authority to obtain it, life in a white world required constant navigation.

Death lingered. He didn't have to pursue it. It stuck around like an impatient teacher waiting for him to finish an impossible exam. Why else would it send another power-mongering white man into his life?

Pyen must have blabbed about how much Jimmy loved museums. It wasn't a coincidence they all stood surrounded by the trapped bones of ancient monsters, his mother's brown fingers entwined in the pasty white hand of a devil. A relationship with the six-foot-tall deputy was insane. White men don't ever really love Indians. Especially not tobacco-chewing-cowboy-boot-wearing-red-necks like Deputy Benson.

Around him, the two-story quarry had three sides constructed of steel and glass. An actual mountain made up the fourth wall. According to the ranger, the rock surface contained over 1,500 scrambled dinosaur remnants.

Jimmy walked down a zig-zag ramp to the quarry's first floor. His mother and her date, who reeked of Old Spice, remained on the open second-floor platform. If he had the power to act on his choices, he would be turning over rocks in Vernal to find Coyote Joe, not escorting his mother into her future hell.

Years of greasy, human hands made the fossils smooth. Jimmy added his prints to the mix, hoping to ease his fears. Pyen stood on the platform above him in more danger than a live T-Rex would cause.

"Are you a real Indian?"

He turned to find a little girl with bright red ringlets pointing at his long black braid with a white feather tied to the end of it. He smiled into the brown eyes that matched his own.

"Yes."

"Do you kill cowboys?"

He laughed. He'd love to kill the one standing by his mother right about now. He didn't say that. Instead he knelt down to her level and said, "Don't believe all the junk you hear about Indians. Okay? I'm Ute."

"Like Utah?"

"Yep. Just like that."

"We're from Ohio. That's an Indian word."

"You're pretty smart."

A shadow appeared over Jimmy's shoulder. Instinct told him to brace himself for a hard fist against his head. In the days when beatings happened regularly, he turned himself into a frozen pond. He pulled all his nerves into the core of his body and made his skin hard. He could take a blow with as much inanimate energy as possible. I'm solid. I'm solid. I'm solid.

But no one hit him. Instead the girl's mother muttered "sorry" and hurried her daughter away. He relaxed and tried to believe the apology, but more than likely the woman didn't want her daughter talking to a stranger with brown skin and a long braid.

Jimmy stood up. This date could end anytime now. He'd come to the dinosaur quarry by emotional force. Pyen revealed she'd been seeing the deputy for six weeks.

An ache pushed against his ribs in time with his pulse.

Six weeks. They'd only been in Vernal for ten.

A mother shouldn't hide things from her own son. Especially not his mother, given their history. He should have realized Pyen might bring home a new "dad." If he could kick himself in the shins right now, he would. A cautious and protective son would have stayed alert. But he'd become absorbed with the nearness of the reservation, he'd stop paying attention to how his mother spent her free time.

He stepped back to distance himself even further from Pyen and the deputy. The white man's eyes were concealed by reflective aviators. Even with the room's brightness, only people with something to hide wore sunglasses inside. If he could find the secret, maybe he could trigger the deputy to show his true colors before the man moved in.

He approached the part of the building made from an actual mountain. On any other day, he would have marveled at a three-sided structure bolted to rock and protruding earth. Today he didn't care—couldn't care—about the scrambled bones entombed in the rock wall.

He had a living predator to worry about. He swallowed hard and tried to slow his pulse. He extended his fingers toward an ancient femur bone. Years of greasy, human hands made the fossil smooth and cool. His panic didn't ease. Pyen continued to stand on the platform above him. He kept her in his peripheral vision. He didn't need to move his head to see her lean against the white man. Pyen had the horrible capacity to attract bad men the way white lint clung to brown corduroy.

Jimmy inched closer to the exit.

The redheaded girl whined, "No, Mommy, I don't wanna."

He turned to see the little girl pull away from the exposed bones in the mountain.

"Sweetheart, it's part of an honest-to-goodness dinosaur."

His fingers drummed a nervous beat against his leg.

Red curls struck the child's cheeks, as she shook her head.

"Come on." The woman dragged the girl closer to the rock wall.

Drum. Drum. Drum.

"We didn't come all this way for you to act like a baby." The mother's grip tightened on the little girl's arm.

"Leave her alone!" Jimmy kinda shouted. He didn't mean for it to echo around the building.

"Excuse me?" The mother glared.

He stole a look back toward the platform. The deputy stared down at him through mirrored glasses. The man's thin lips drew a straight line under a caterpillar mustache. Pyen pointed her thick, brown finger in another direction. The white man's mouth answered her, but his focus remained fixed on Jimmy.

Outside the window, a cloud darkened the room.

The deputy's presence shrunk the building to the size of a shoebox.

He stepped out of view. Panic punched his heart to beat faster. In a distant part of his brain, he knew his reaction was over the top. Something the army counselors called post-traumatic stress. But logic and understanding didn't dispel the fear.

Dad's dead. He reminded himself.

The ranger next to him scowled.

Dad's dead. He leaned against the farthest wall out of the deputy's line of sight.

A group of tourists spit out unrecognizable syllables.

Dad's dead. The mantra usually helped, but not today. He hadn't seen a counselor since before Drunk Dean moved in with them, but he knew PTSD didn't just go away.

In front of him, the ringleted girl trembled. Her angry mother leaned over and whispered into the girl's ear. Tears rimmed the small brown eyes. More than a dozen people wandered around. No intervention. No help.

Fear knotted in his gut and forced its way up his throat. The stale air in the room crowded his lungs. But like a quadrillion other times in his life, he couldn't move. He wanted to speak up. Risk injury today to avoid months of it later.

"Fine, you can sit in the car!" the redhead's mother growled. With a vice-like grip on the girl's arm, the woman led her through the exit and out of sight.

Tension and panic and yuck wormed its way through his heart. He scratched at his jeans with his stubby nails. He would love to disappear and forget about the whole scene, but he knew when his fear left, failure would weigh on him. He didn't want that. He was already responsible for a war's worth of dead. He longed for the power to stop all the flinching and do something.

Besides, right now, no leather belt dangled in an angry fist. Instead, a frightened little girl was learning to fear more than dinosaurs. She had trembled at the tone in her mother's voice. Even with Deputy Benson stalking the quarry, he had to act.

"Come on!" he mumbled to himself. He counted to ten and blew a heavy breath.

The ranger stared at him.

"What?" Jimmy challenged. Not loud enough to awaken the monster upstairs, but enough to make his point. "You never see an Indian brave?"

The man pulled his head back in surprise. Jimmy hurried out of the exit before anything or anyone else could stop him.

CHAPTER 15

Q: *Could dinosaurs live in extreme heat?*
A: *Many reptiles live in hot arid climates.*

The bright sun assaulted him as soon as he left the air-conditioned quarry. Jimmy didn't have an actual plan. He paced past the mother and her distraught child. With his hands on his head, he kept his back to them and dropped his jaw wide and inhaled.

What would he say? He plopped his arms down. What could he say? He fumbled in his pocket for an answer. A gift of some kind to distract the girl from her fear. He pulled out a bunch of nothing.

Two crumpled dollars.

His cellphone.

A quarter, four pennies and a nickel.

His other pocket held his rabbit-foot key chain and Swiss Army knife.

None of that would bring a smile to a frightened spirit.

An open-air van wobbled around the quarry's mountain. The shuttle carried tourists back and forth to the visitors parking lot a half a mile down the hill. He didn't have much time. If he didn't act, the moment would escape him.

The air brakes gasped.

Three tourists climbed off the shuttle.

Think, Jimmy, think. He shoved a well-gnawed fingernail into his mouth.

"Sure, is nice out." A woman paused at the front step.

"Yes, ma'am, it is." The driver nodded. "Enjoy the quarry."

The man behind the wheel was Ute. Although he didn't wear his hair in a long braid like Jimmy, the round face and dark skin gave it away. The twenty-something brother gave him a nod. A sign of acknowledgment reserved for brown people. A note to say, we're in this together. Across the country, the same "how ya doin" was shared by hundreds of dark-skinned people. Bonded by trials at the unfair hands of whites.

The gesture reminded Jimmy of the woven band around his ankle. He'd braided it less than a week ago, so the anklet hadn't become too grungy to be given away.

An old woman crept toward the van. Her ancient husband stood behind her. Besides the old man, six other passengers, and the little redhead and her mother.

Jimmy lowered himself to one knee.

The old man handed his wife her cane and ambled up the steps.

He fumbled with the strings long enough to know he'd need an hour to untie them. Come on. He couldn't wait that long. Standing again, he retrieved his pocketknife.

He felt the little girl's curiosity as he sawed the threads. He glanced up. She was leaning against her mother's leg. When he caught her eye, she didn't shy away. Without fear, she watched him. He chose a place that would allow the girl to tie the band again.

He couldn't stand seeing a parent humiliate a child. The shift in the girl's demeanor. The change of power. Like a bully wielding anger like a stick. An ugliness stirred inside him. The anger made him feel too much like his father's son. He never wanted rage to motivate him.

Crap.

The friendship band broke free.

The mother pulled her daughter into the van.

He folded his knife and stood at the shuttle door. He had no idea if his plan would work. The mother might refuse the gift. The other adults might chase him away or remember seeing the deputy's uniform inside and invite the real danger to join the party.

The girl sat with her back toward Jimmy.

He couldn't move.

His breathing became choppy.

The small gift hung limp. Even the wind waited in anticipation.

"Maiku." The driver nodded to him.

He lifted his hand to receive the Ute greeting. He'd never heard anyone but Pyen say it.

"You getting on?"

Jimmy wanted to. He wanted to escape. He wanted to have this Ute drive the shuttle all the way to the rez. If he made friends with this guy, he wouldn't need to hunt for Coyote Joe. But the driver was obviously a token Indian with a white-man's uniform. Another Indian who loved white men just like Pyen. And the thought of leaving Pyen alone with the deputy hurt deeper than his heart.

Ten pairs of eyeballs studied him, including the child with the red ringlets.

He shook his head. The action rattled his tongue loose. "I want to give the little girl something."

A sweet "aww" came from the lips of the old lady.

The mother squinted at him with suspicion.

The old man frowned. No doubt, he questioned Jimmy's long black hair, tied in a traditional Indian braid at the back of his head. Whatever. Let them think what they want. He had to be brave.

"I want to tell her she doesn't have to be afraid of dinosaurs."

He extended his arm. The woven, blue and brown thread dangled from his fingers. A simple bracelet might not make a little red-headed girl smile. But if her life contained the kind of violence his had, death would be the only solution. The grave conquered more than dinosaurs. It defeated people too.

"Go on, take it." The older lady nodded at the mother.

He didn't expect the woman to listen, let alone smile. But both of those things happened before he could respond to his urge to run. The bracelet was taken. His plan worked. It had actually worked. The little girl smiled.

Jimmy backed out of the shuttle and the driver pulled away. He decided not to blame the mother. She was probably married to a man whose white face turned red moments before his fists clenched.

The little girl waved at him until the van rounded the mountain wall.

A sense of limbo surrounded him, the odd combination of satisfaction and nothing-really-changes reality. He might have brought a mother and daughter a little closer, but a bigger problem roamed the quarry behind him, clutching Pyen's hand.

Pain lurked in his past that didn't need resurrecting. Old answered prayers that killed off each danger one by one. Eliminating the threat of injury forever. Or so he thought.

Why would Pyen ever date another one of those savages? The worst thing in life would be to have a new dad. Especially a white one. He never wanted to feel the sting of leather against his bare skin again.

The Uintah Basin stretched out around him. Across the brown hills, the reservation called to him. The victory he'd just accomplished drove his desire to solve the biggest problem facing him. He would solve his white-man dilemma with action, not frozen like a totem. The breeze brushed a whiff of mountain sage across his face. The arid sun spoke to him. He would get Pyen safely to the reservation with the help of Coyote Joe.

The old man's friends had camping gear and Jimmy could no longer wait until the powwow.

CHAPTER 16

Q: *Which dinosaur was the most violent?*
A: *T. rex is considered the most powerful of the meat-eaters. Also, on the list is the Utahraptor with its sharp teeth and a huge killer toe.*

Jimmy paced the quarry's curved sidewalk. Gray clouds reared back into angry fists. The weatherman threatened rain and the sky appeared tough enough to obey. But a refreshing storm would probably only hang in the teasing sky. He bit down on a chewed-up thumbnail. Across the river, sprinklers circled cow-speckled fields. How different would this land have looked two centuries ago? The irrigated green would have remained a proper shade of earth. But white men eradicated brown whenever they found it.

This land should still be part of the Uintah and Ouray reservation. Of course, the boundaries for that land had been rubbed indecipherable by the lies of a white government. He didn't care. The brown hills, dotted with high-desert junipers, called to him like a wolf yelping for her missing pups. He needed to find Coyote Joe.

The thump of cowboy boots landed on the concrete behind him accompanied by the aggressive scent of Old Spice.

"What are you doing out here?"

Jimmy swung around. The blond caterpillar above the devil's upper lip twitched. His pronounced jaw remained firm. Even after an hour of sightseeing, the starched lines of his uniform remained stiff and tight.

"Truthfully?"

"Of course." The deputy chuckled.

"I was getting away from you."

"Jimmy." Pyen frowned and shook her head.

"It's okay." The white man grinned. "Give him time."

Pyen's flat Ute features smiled up at the tall white man. Then she leaned her round body into his. Jimmy's heart sank. She trusted the devil. Her eyes glossed over, blinding her to any danger. His mother reached a hand toward him. She wanted to pull him into what she believed would be a happy family.

He folded his arms.

Deputy Benson aimed his keys at an oversized pickup. The locks responded with a double click. The white man didn't ride the shuttle. Instead, he parked in the quarry's private lot. Regular people, like Jimmy, had to leave their cars at the visitor center half a mile below. He tucked his head in shame as he passed people waiting in the high desert heat for a ride.

"What's next?" The man of privilege smiled at Pyen. He looked like a T. rex eyeing a vulnerable Protoscerotops.

"Jimmy's going to visit his friend Devin in Jensen." Pyen nodded at him.

"No, I'm not." Jimmy climbed behind the passenger seat into the extended cab and buckled his seat belt. He had promised to meet Devin's grandparents, but he couldn't retreat now. Based on the sickening glow on his mother's face, he needed to get into town. He needed to find his birth certificate and Coyote Joe. Forget about politics. The elders couldn't refuse to rescue him and Pyen.

"Changed your mind?" The deputy's voice deepened. His sunglasses concealed the man's eyes like the film on a sleeping serpent.

"Homework." Jimmy stiffened but maintained eye contact. Only stupid people turned away from a snake.

"But school's over," Pyen said.

The deputy stretched his lips into a tight grin.

Jimmy squeezed his fingers against his leg. "Summer project." He tightened his grip, to keep the anxiety from reaching up to his face. "For science class."

The deputy's smile lingered. Having been raised by a violent and cunning white man, Jimmy recognized the tension behind a smile. The deputy probably knew Jimmy lied. The devil sought to squirm deeper into his head like an earwig. "The quarry must have inspired you then."

"Something like that."

"That's wonderful." Pyen beamed. She missed all the hints. Although reflective lens masked the man's eyes, the monster gave it away in the curl of his lips. Years ago, when Pyen didn't take her eyes off her feet, the beast used to promise his family a movie or baseball game or trip to the moon. When the offer was a set-up, his father's lip would twitch on the right side.

Deputy Benson didn't twitch, but the tight-lipped grin sent a recognizable prickle through Jimmy's skin. The extended cab felt suddenly small, the reek of cheap cologne choking the air. Impending trouble rose in the confined space, invisible yet tangible. With meteorological skill, Jimmy knew a violent storm would soon batter their world. Intuition was hard to explain, but instinct shouted. This man had an ugly plan. And it would be unfurled within the hour.

He fought back a desire to roll down the window and hurl himself to the pavement. Escape would release the building pressure in his chest. But he wouldn't. Not today. He had to stick around and watch this guy. He squeezed his leg and tried to stay calm. They continued along Brush Creek Road until they reached the landfill. The deputy turned left onto 500 North. The tension accelerated as they roared down into Vernal. Whatever lay ahead could change everything. He would be in this man's business until the devil left Pyen alone. Whatever the white man had planned, Jimmy would be in the way.

Once he had his birth certificate, Coyote Joe could take him to the reservation. They'd have to offer shelter to him. He's Ute.

The cell phone in Jimmy's pocket vibrated. He fumbled to retrieve it without unbuckling his seatbelt. The deputy pointed to a house on the side of the road, some friend of the man. Pyen nodded and smiled.

He checked his phone. Devin's name appeared on the screen next to a text, "u comin?"

Jimmy's fingers bounced along the keypad. "Can't."

"Why?"

"LATER!" He texted and stuffed the phone back into his pocket.

Deputy Benson adjusted the rearview mirror until the reflective surface framed his sunglass-covered eyes. Jimmy couldn't see the devil's grin in the glass but noticed from the back seat the skin wrinkle beside his right eye. A subtle smoke signal. Jimmy accepted the warning. Whatever the deputy had planned, at least Jimmy wouldn't be caught off guard. He'd stay alert. This early in the relationship, the white man would be subversive. A show of power without being violent. Jimmy overheard Pyen's first boyfriend tell a buddy he'd rigged the car engine to smoke. Pyen freaked out, but then the jerk played the loving hero and fixed it. Those moments kept his mother confused enough to forgive. She always believed the white man's games.

Deputy Benson's Ford F250 slowed before turning right into Fairview Trailer Park. Five hundred yards from their trailer, Jimmy unbuckled his seat belt. He might be trapped without back doors, but at least not tied to the seat.

Before he could brace himself, the deputy slammed on his brakes.

Gravel clapped against the floorboard.

Jimmy's head crashed into the back of the front passenger seat.

His butt slid to the floorboard.

Pyen gasped.

Her shoulder strap snapped as it constrained her to the seat.

"Stay here!" the deputy shouted. The driver's door clicked open then slammed shut.

Jimmy bit back every swear word Pyen didn't know he knew. He'd let his guard down. This white man was crafty. No time to get angry. The moment he anticipated had come. From his elbows, he lifted himself off the floor. Leaning between the front bucket seats he asked, "Pyen, you okay?"

"Paa, look." He wished he really was water. He would turn into a river and pull his mother as far away from the trouble outside the windshield as possible.

Their living-room window gaped like an open sore.

The air conditioner lay cracked and broken on the ground. When they left it had been nestled in the frame.

Deputy Benson crept toward the house with his gun drawn.

"Who would do this?" Pyen whispered.

The deputy topped his list of suspects, but he kept that to himself. The white man must have paid someone to break in. He could have timed it so that no one else would investigate before he arrived. His rescue and concern could make a weak woman scared to live without him. A regular white knight.

With no doors to help him escape the back seat, he crawled between the two front seats and eased his way behind the steering wheel.

The crafty deputy crept toward a tree, hidden from the trailer, but as visible as a drive-in movie through the windshield. The whole scene played perfectly into the white man's hands. The kind of manipulation devils used to gain the trust of unsuspecting Indians.

And from the look on Pyen's face, the scam worked.

Jimmy knew better. No one would scope out the rundown trailer park. Even a crackhead could tell the place had nothing to steal. Everyone in the park used food stamps.

The sun cast crooked shadows from cottonwood branches. The pressure around them couldn't be seen. The tight air sucked away any sound. Definitely a set-up. Normally, the German shepherd in the first trailer barked its head off at the slightest thing.

He turned off the air conditioner and rolled down all the windows.

The engine from the white man's truck idled.

He leaned his head outside.

Not a single woof from the noisy dog. The canine must sense the trouble. Not the kind of trouble that put you in detention.

The heavy, thin air meant the mean-ugly-violent kind of trouble.

"What are you doing?" Pyen's voice trembled.

"Shhh."

A light breeze carried in fumes from the exhaust.

"What's going on?"

He held his index finger to his lips. She obeyed.

Gloomy trailers lined both sides of the drive. On the left, red sheets covered the windows in a blue single-wide. The next mobile home had a torn screen where faded sunflowers waved slowly back and forth. Step by step, the deputy passed by rusted paneling and broken stairs.

"Look," Pyen pointed.

A shadow shifted in his mother's bedroom window.

The accomplice still rummaged through the house.

His mother leaned over and pressed the horn.

The blast made the deputy jump. The shadow inside dropped out of sight.

"Stop it."

"I need to warn him." She honked the horn again.

"Don't." He pulled her hand away. This time he kept it caged in his fist.

"He could get hurt."

"That's not our problem." He hissed at her. She was wrong again. So very, very, very wrong. Her self-destructive love life couldn't be more wrong. For the first time in his entire life he wanted to slap her. He wanted to shake her until her eyes wobbled in her skull. The surge of emotion shocked him.

He released her hand.

Never. Never. Never.

He couldn't let anything or anyone ever take him there.

Outside, Deputy Benson scrambled to the house and crouched below the window. He waved his hand toward them, a signal to drive away. Jimmy didn't care about the set up anymore. If the devil wanted them to go, they would comply. The bad energy in the air made the decision easy. Besides, Pyen didn't need to witness this hero show a minute longer.

Jimmy shifted the truck into reverse. He'd learned to drive back in Washington. He didn't have a license, but this wasn't the time to worry about that.

"What are you doing?"

"Getting out of here."

"You can't leave Andrew behind."

"Ohhhh, yes, I can."

"What if he gets hurt?"

Jimmy didn't answer. His heart beat against his ribs like a baseball bat. He couldn't believe Pyen cared so much about someone who would probably beat her every day. He squealed the truck around. Dust and exhaust invaded the cab.

At the front trailer, the formerly mute German shepherd barked.

As he pulled the truck out of the lot, the crack of a gun sounded in the trailer park behind them.

CHAPTER 17

Q: *Could dinosaurs fly?*
A: *No. Animals like Pterosaurs are considered cousins to the dinosaurs.*

"Turn around." Panic elevated Pyen's voice. "Turn around. Turn around."

"He's a cop," Jimmy shouted. "He can take care of himself."

"I heard a gunshot."

He didn't want to tell his mother what he'd seen from the rearview mirror. The deputy didn't shoot at a criminal. The devil stood up and aimed the gun at a wood pile and fired.

"Don't worry."

"What if he's hurt?"

The big Ford squealed around the corner.

The white man wasn't in danger, they were. His intuition nailed it. The shadow in the house had been hired. The devil set up the whole thing. A fancy act to scare Jimmy and Pyen into trusting the deputy.

But he wouldn't get away with it. The Vernal police station was around the corner on Main Street near the museum. The deputy might not accuse Jimmy of stealing his truck, not with Pyen as a witness, but better to get rid of it as soon as possible. The deputy planned to trap and control her like Dad had. White men loved control.

Jimmy couldn't fix any of that until he got to the reservation. And that meant finding Coyote Joe. The old man might be anywhere. Before he could look, he needed to report the break-in. Put it on record for real. At least then, the deputy wouldn't be able to pretend to handle it. Jimmy would get a legitimate police record, make a copy for himself and give an extra to Devin. Something a TV judge called an evidence file.

He parked the truck in the station parking lot. "Let's go, Pyen."

"Where?" Her eyes glossed over. The scene affected her more than he liked. No doubt the gunshot. Stupid deputy.

The sun heated the air in the cab. Her shoulders slumped. Jimmy didn't want her to be alone. She deserved a husband who would care for her and protect her. Not the manipulative antics of a white man. "It's okay. We're going into the police station. Get some help."

She stared at the windshield confused.

"Pyen." He squeezed her hand. "It'll be all right."

He got out of the car and slammed the door. They needed to go back to the reservation together. To be back with their own people. If Pyen wanted a husband, she could find one there. He crossed the front of the truck to the passenger side. The white deputy wouldn't do. The crafty devil was already ten steps ahead of him. Jimmy's heart hurt as he remembered Pyen said they'd been dating for six weeks. Long enough for the creep to have Jimmy followed.

The thought brought Jimmy to a full stop.

Surveillance.

Maybe even cameras.

Did the deputy know about Coyote Joe?

The skin on his arms prickled even though the sun blazed in the sky.

The homeless warrior could be in as much danger as he and Pyen. The squealing image of an allosaurus statue at the Field House skulked into his mind. How many more people would he need to rescue from danger?

Opening his mother's door, he reminded himself he could

only help one person at a time.

"Come on, Pyen." He gave her his hand. She climbed out like she was eighty years old.

He hesitated at the station door. Exit routes were more obvious in the fresh air. But no one would come out to him. He had to go inside. After a couple deep breaths, he pushed past his anxiety and into the building. His heart pounded harder than he liked. In front of him, a Plexiglas window separated him from two women dressed in regular clothes. No one around him wore a uniform. Without looking up, one of the women said, "Can I help you?"

"We need to report a break-in."

"When did it happen?"

"Right now."

"What do you mean?" The woman stopped typing and looked up.

"I mean," He bit back any sarcasm. He needed these white people. The idea made his stomach lurch. Not a good position for an Indian to find himself. But until he could get to the reservation and his own people, he was stuck. "There's someone in our house right now."

"Where do you live?"

"Fairview Trailer Park." Pyen spoke up.

"I'll get an officer."

"We'll wait outside." The lady eyed Jimmy suspiciously. "My mother's had a shock, she needs fresh air."

He found a shady spot and had Pyen sit down on the cement steps. He went back to the truck and got her a bottle of water. Cars full of white people sped past them. The Stars and Stripes flapped above them. A western wind snapped the flag. That same breeze would have passed over the reservation. He was closer than he'd ever been to a place with mostly brown people. His people.

Pyen trembled.

Before he could reassure her, a blond officer approached.

"We've sent a cruiser to the trailer park." He put his hands on his hips. "What can you tell me?"

"Deputy Benson is over there! Please, please, you need to

help him." Pyen panted. Jimmy rubbed her shoulder while the officer got on his radio.

"Hey, Karl, Deputy Benson is on the scene. Over."

"Great." The voice crackled over the radio. "All we need is that whack job around. The man is a menace. They should have taken away his badge and gun after he —"

The young officer fumbled with the radio before successfully clicking it off.

Jimmy held his breath. The cop smiled, but white people smiled too much.

"Let me get some basic information."

"No," Jimmy said. "Why don't you tell me what that was about?"

"That?" The cop blinked a million times and swallowed. "Just an inside joke."

He didn't push it. But he knew better, Deputy Benson wasn't a joke. Intuition like his cut both ways. His radar screamed from the moment they met. The white man was dangerous. Now his fellow officers confirmed it. Coyote Joe needed to be found before the deputy could get to him. The crazy, white man had probably been stalking them the whole time. He might even know about Coyote Joe's dumpster dives and Jimmy's willingness to take the old Indian home for a free meal. Jimmy rubbed his forehead hoping to erase his regrets.

The officer jotted down their names and address first. Jimmy let Pyen do most of the talking. It seemed to settle her. She began to ramble a bit. To the cop's credit, he didn't look bored while she started with the "wonderful day at the quarry." Jimmy nodded at the appropriate times while checking his watch. Every minute should be spent on finding and warning Coyote Joe.

"Okay, young man," The officer turned to Jimmy. "What do you remember?"

He recounted everything he'd seen, including the gunshot.

The officer turned pale.

"Excuse me a second." The man walked away so he could use his radio in private.

Maybe this white guy would help them.

Maybe they'd arrest the deputy.

Then again maybe the Mojave Desert would get snow this year.

The officer returned with another wide smile painted on his white face. "Looks like they've apprehended the suspect."

"Is Andrew all right?"

"Come on, Pyen, didn't you hear the man say the deputy is crazy?"

"I didn't say that."

Jimmy didn't shake his head, but he wanted to. He had bigger things to deal with than white men protecting white men. He needed to draw his mother out of shock. He needed her to hear from other sources about the risks she was taking. "This man you're dating is dangerous."

"No." She stared at the bush beside them.

"Tell her," he said directly to the cop. "Tell her the kind of man she's dealing with."

"I really can't get involved."

"You're already involved."

His radio hummed and a crackling voice came over the speaker, "We're pulling in now. Suspect in custody."

"Is the deputy with you?"

The cop walked toward the driveway as the cruiser pulled in.

Deputy Benson sat in the passenger seat and Jimmy wanted to vomit. He refused to stick around while the demon arrived with his fake perp. The gloating. The heroics. The yuck.

"Andrew." The vulnerability in his mother's voice made it worse.

"Deputy Benson will be here in a moment, ma'am." The officer helped. "Let's go inside and get you some more water."

"Thanks," Jimmy said it and meant it. He'd long ago discovered what any person of color knew in moments like this. Not all devils are equal. He didn't trust the Vernal cop any more than he trusted Deputy Benson. But for now, he put his disgust aside for the bigger goal.

Pyen would have to be rescued by a fake hero this time. At least the police were fully aware of all of today's bizarre behavior. Next step, find Coyote Joe. White people have no clue. They think that because an Indian smiles or nods his head that they are in agreement. Burying true thoughts comes as natural to brown-skinned people as getting a tan.

He began to follow them into the building when Deputy Benson emerged from the black police cruiser. The creep lifted his hand in a robotic wave.

Jimmy tightened his arms to his side. He tried to keep his jaw tight as well but found it difficult when the cop on the other side released the prisoner from the back seat.

Coyote Joe made eye contact with Jimmy and grimaced.

CHAPTER 18

Q: *How much did a Stegosaurus weigh?*
A: *About two tons with a broad, thick body.*

After the dust settled, Jimmy did the hardest thing ever. He left Pyen at the police station locked in the "there-there" hug of Demon Benson. The deputy was a liar. Nothing about this crap was "going to be all right."

He resurrected his previous lie. "I'm going to the library to work on my summer project."

The deputy didn't move and Pyen didn't try to stop Jimmy. And all of that stung. The many memories of rejection from childhood pooled together and tugged at him. He jaywalked across Highway 40. Coyote Joe was captured and it was all his fault. The old man didn't deserve to be locked up by the whack job. Come on. The deputy snatched the man's freedom while scheming to steal Pyen's life. If the white man had his way, everyone Jimmy knew would be locked up in some way or another.

The old Indian wasn't the target, yet he was the one locked up. If Jimmy could have changed places with Coyote Joe, he would have. He didn't feel sorry for himself and he wasn't acting all noble. The old guy appeared on the deputy's radar because he showed up on Jimmy's. The whole crime was too staged to be an accident. The entire arrest, too convenient.

Inside the library, Jimmy wandered around touching books without reading titles. Stories locked in time. Words unable to change. Endings on pages already decided. A couple month ago, Jimmy would have sunk into a world of sweets and fried foods. Instead, he pulled a book from the shelf. White people wrote all the stories.

White people controlled all the endings.

He wanted more than anything to be touching books and words written by Utes. To reach into the future and find a story true to his life.

After he dropped the book on a table, he sat down in front of a computer. He Googled Ute Indian and found their official website. But it didn't provide information about what to expect if he went alone. No invitation to come talk to the elders.

A click on the back arrow brought him to Google again. He typed in, "Ute Indian FAQ." He learned the frequently-asked-question trick from a black kid he knew in Washington. The Utah Division of Indian Affairs came up number two. A memory wrestled its way back into his mind.

Dad with a can of Coors in his hand announcing, "All Indians are government-leeching drunks." Stupid idiot. According to FAQ on the UDIA website, Indians paid taxes unless they lived and worked on the reservation. Government resources were limited.

He knew it. Knew the beast was wrong on a hundred levels. But, one fact on the site sunk his heart. For years he'd considered himself more Ute than white. A true member of the tribe with location being the only thing lacking. But a major problem glared at him from the screen.

"The Ute Indian Tribe of Utah has one of the highest quantum requirements: five-eighths Ute Indian blood."

Jimmy was a master at math. And without jotting down a single number he knew that Five-eighths was more than fifty percent. His breath caught in his throat. This couldn't be. Unless Dad had some Ute blood, Jimmy could only be fifty-fifty at best.

He swallowed.

He wasn't Ute enough.

The shock was thick and solid in his chest. The ache was real, as if someone drove a redneck pickup directly into his ribcage. He couldn't go to the reservation by himself, birth certificate or not. The whiteness of his father cursed him deeper than he ever imagined. Rejection from the tribal elders was guaranteed. All thoughts of storming his way into his homeland and demanding help became infantile. The childish dreams of a half-breed.

Not wanted by whites.

Not wanted by Indians.

The idea ate at his brain cells. It pushed tears into the back of his eyes and a hard lump into the center of his throat. The entire white world rejected him and now it was very possible so would his tribe. The isolation of no-mans-land surrounded him. And the saddest part of it all was, it had always been true. He'd always been only half and half and belonging to neither.

He placed his hands on the table to steady himself. This couldn't be the end. He forced himself to breathe. There had to be more options than this. He stared at the screen without seeing the images. He had to hope they cared enough about the loss of a full-blooded daughter to get involved.

The walls of the library boxed him in.

He shut down the website.

Coyote Joe was locked in jail. Probably because of his relationship with Jimmy. Probably because he was the one man who would have helped rescue Pyen from a demon deputy. This couldn't be the end of the old man. But it would be the death of their friendship. Once the old Indian was released, he'd want nothing more to do with Jimmy.

He rounded the checkout desk and left the building.

The white light of the summer sun hurt his eyes. Maybe he could meet Coyote Joe at the jail, get a letter from him or something. But Deputy Benson would find out about any and every visitor at the jail. In fact, the white devil would hope Jimmy would go, then spin lies about Jimmy to Pyen. No man had ever been able to separate him from his mother. But this man did get her to date him secretly for six weeks.

Jimmy would have to go to the reservation alone and prove

himself. According to the old warrior, that could take months, years. Time he didn't have.

He picked up a stick and let it thump against random trees as he walked home. If he stayed in Vernal, he'd end up in jail. The deputy had powers bigger than Jimmy's real father ever had. Not just a fist, but a gun and a badge.

Regardless of his limited blood lineage, he had to get to the reservation. If they rejected him, he'd make them understand they'd be killing Pyen. He had no other choice. He couldn't survive if he sat back and watched his mother destroy herself. At least not when an option remained untried.

The reservation had its own laws. The deputy had no jurisdiction there. He knew his mother should have never left. She would have been safer among her own people. He could have been born for this purpose alone.

No other choice but to go.

He walked up the street with a straighter posture than when he'd started.

The June sky burned like an August afternoon. He smiled in spite of the circumstances. The deputy would never successfully rob him of his connection to this basin. His one-mile walk home stirred his strength. And even if he was only four-eighths Ute, his heart thumped a full eight-eighths. If one-eighth kept him from gaining membership, it would never make what his father said true.

It no longer mattered that Google Maps listed twenty-four miles to Fort Duchesne. His mind returned to the thrill of the bus ride from Salt Lake to Vernal. Back then, the crisp, dry air whipped against his hair as Pyen hid her face from the Bottle Hollow turn off. He had never had the chance to take that road. Now, he would be on that road before nightfall.

He'd go today. Without Coyote Joe and without Pyen.

CHAPTER 19

Q: *Could dinosaurs see in the dark?*
A: *Evidence presented by scientists at the University of California, Davis studied the scleral ring on dinosaurs and living lizards indicating the possibility of night vision.*

The gravel in the trailer-park's driveway remained chewed up where Jimmy had gunned it earlier. The German shepherd greeted him with an open-jawed bark, tail wagging behind him. "I'm getting my stuff and getting out of here, boy," he said to the dog and gave him a salute. He had never run away from home before. He'd always been too afraid to leave Pyen. But he needed to leave now if he was ever going to save her from the deputy.

Twenty feet further into the trailer park his heart sank. The deputy's Ford sat next to the trailer. The broken air conditioner now lay in the bed of the truck. The window was still open. The smell of Old Spice strangled the fresh air. He didn't want to go in, but he'd never get to the reservation without a little cash and his bike. To make sure he wasn't followed, he'd have to wait for the snake to slither away.

Inside, Pyen and the deputy sat at the dining room table. The white man's big frame clogged the room, making it hard for Jimmy to breathe.

"Oh, Paa," His mother stood and hugged him. "I'm so glad you're home. I don't like all this trouble."

"I'm fine." He patted her back.

"Come over and see." She pulled him by the hand. "Andrew has some pictures."

Deputy Benson slid two pieces of paper across Pyen's dining room table. Each page contained the mug shots of six men. "Do you recognize anyone?"

Jimmy wiped the back of his hand against his moist forehead. "No." He tried hard not to look at Coyote Joe's face longer than the others. How much did the deputy already know and how much was just fishing?

The whack-job leaned back. Without his sunglasses, the white man's eyes were two different colors. One brown and the other a blue so pale it blended into the white of his eye. The black pupil stared out like a laser. Jimmy didn't think it possible, but the man's face scared him more without the sunglasses.

The blue curtains floated back and forth in the occasional breeze from the broken window. The leather fringe from the bear-dance costume Pyen wore as a child fluttered. The deputy would probably imprison the free movement of the wind before he left. Whatever, Jimmy wouldn't be here to see it. The demon leaned his elbows on the table, arms overlapping each other.

Jimmy stretched his feet under the table. The tips of his fingers turned cold. The muffled voices of nosy neighbors snuck in with the breeze. While their gossipy ways annoyed him, the fresh air helped relieve his nostrils of the pungent smell of Old Spice.

"Son," The white man couldn't have used a more alienating term. "There's nothing to be afraid of."

Jimmy bounced the tips of his shoes together.

"Listen," The deputy's voice softened. The condescending tone reminded Jimmy of his elementary school principal. "The man who broke in claims he knows you."

Jimmy didn't look up. He picked up the papers as if he needed a closer look. The devil knew something. Coyote Joe wouldn't have ratted Jimmy out, but there could be no harm in admitting he'd bumped into the old man. "He looks like a homeless man I met at the dinosaur museum." Jimmy pointed at Coyote Joe. "Didn't I see him in the back of the police car with you?"

The deputy's eyes narrowed.

The white man preferred to do the questioning.

Jimmy folded his arms and continued to knock his feet together. Certain facts would never be shared. Especially about bringing the hungry man home. The intrusive deputy might already know everything, with cameras and surveillance, but he'd have to admit to following Jimmy and that would blow the creep's cover.

He wondered how the deputy had frightened Coyote Joe enough to make him break into the trailer. The white man must have used force against the old warrior.

"You trust this man?" Deputy Benson questioned.

"I don't know him like that."

"You only met at the museum?"

"As far as I remember."

"He's dangerous, you know."

Not as dangerous as you.

"He's a known drug addict."

Whatever. That might be the lie the deputy wanted Pyen to believe, but cops plant drugs on people all the time. In fact, the deputy, no doubt, planted drugs on the old man to blackmail him. That would be enough to trap an Indian.

Jimmy's heart hurt. This was all his fault. The only reason Coyote Joe had to deal with the deputy was because Jimmy made friends with him. A Taco Bell dumpster had to be more comfortable than Vernal City jail. But how could he have known at the time the devil followed him? The whack-job deputy wanted Pyen. To accomplish that, he would eliminate the adults they knew first. Isolation. The white man's first stage of control.

Jimmy sat up and placed his hands on the table. "Can I go to my room now?"

"Sure," Pyen reached over to grab Jimmy's hand, but he stood up and pulled it away before she could touch him. She was partly to blame for this whole mess.

"One more thing."

Jimmy sighed but didn't sit back down.

Deputy Benson reached into his duffle bag and pulled out a PlayStation Portable. Faded dinosaur stickers confirmed his ownership. The deputy shook it to make his point. "This man is not your friend. He stole your property. I caught him climbing out of your bedroom window."

He didn't believe the old man stole the game any more than he believed Deputy Benson's straight white teeth were natural. Jimmy reached out his hand to take his property, only to have the white man pull it back.

"I can't return the evidence yet."

"Shouldn't it be in a plastic bag? Aren't you getting your prints all over it?"

The deputy pulled back his neck until his chin doubled. The white man looked at Pyen. His voice sounded defensive and pleading. "I touched it when I took it from the man."

"Why bring it?" Jimmy pushed.

"I needed to show you." The deputy regained his composure and squinted. "Look, hanging out with a man like this is extremely dangerous."

A slip. "Who said we hung out?" The stalker had to admit to following him in order to bring up how many times Jimmy had met Coyote Joe. He leaned on one leg, strengthened by the shift in power, and stared into the white-blue of Deputy Benson's disgusting eye.

"Just an expression." The devil leaned back.

"Hmm. Here's another expression." Jimmy lifted the edges of his lips into a fake smile. "I'll be in my room." He turned and didn't breathe again until he'd closed his bedroom door behind him.

CHAPTER 20

Q: Did dinosaurs make sounds?
A: Probably. The Lambeosaurus had crests on top of their heads like nostrils. Air could have pushed through these crests and made a deep bellowing sound similar to a horn.

Stupid deputy.

Jimmy paced the floor.

What a jerk. What a tool. What complete and utter . . . Wait a minute.

Since his weight loss, he'd kept his room tidy. It was part of the distractions he used to replace cravings. Vacuum instead of eating. Make the bed instead of munch. Put things away instead of binge. It worked. Problem was, his room was just as clean as when he left it. Nothing was missing. No burglary-tossed clothes. His untouched belongings confirmed the demon didn't bribe Coyote Joe to rob the place.

Everything started to fall into place. If Jimmy had to guess, it was easier to picture the old man coming by to visit, only to find the air conditioner on the ground. He would have come inside to save Jimmy. Instead he probably chased the deputy's accomplice away. That was it. It had to be. Besides, the deputy would have made a bigger mess, a scarier scene.

Coyote Joe had simply been in the wrong place at the wrong

time. Jimmy smiled and exhaled doubt about the old man he didn't know he'd been feeling. The mind could trick a person. For now, Jimmy chose to believe that the deputy hired someone to frighten Pyen, but like all bad-guy plans, an unexpected snag transpired. That would be Coyote Joe. The real creep ran away. When the three of them pulled up in the truck, the old man was inside. The deputy arrested the homeless Indian and took the PlayStation himself and let his accomplice go. The game hadn't been played in months. In fact, Jimmy kept it in the top drawer of his dresser with his Ute scrapbook and the list. It wasn't lying around for a random crook to find and steal.

But wait a minute. The demon couldn't know that without eyes in the room.

Eyes in the house.

Disgusting mismatched eyes on every aspect of Jimmy's life. Yuck. All this time he'd imagined that the demon might have been following him. In fact, he even thought about surveillance. But not until this moment did he think that his own room was bugged.

As casually as possible, he scanned the room and found the hidden camera within seconds. He knew what he owned. The bowling ball. A wooden box with spools of string. Hand weights. A couple new dinosaur posters and a dream catcher hung on the wall. Next to them was something he didn't own. A smoke alarm. On the wall, not the ceiling. The perfect place to hide a camera. Right at eye-level with Jimmy.

A beady-black lens and flashing-red light watched him right now.

Creepy.

He wanted to climb out the window Coyote Joe escaped from earlier. But that would only play into the deputy's hand. No, he could trick the stupid idiot more if he walked out the front door.

Jimmy swallowed.

That's what he'd do. Walk right out the front door with Pyen and her stupid boyfriend watching.

Knowing he was being recorded, he straightened the covers on the bed and tightened the corners. He could say Devin called to meet him, then leave the deputy with Pyen without raising suspicion. He looked at his phone and pretended to respond to a text. He didn't hide the smile as he acted out this fake routine. He could still run away. He could still get to the rez and save Pyen from danger. She'd be okay for a couple of days. She had to be. Time for her to protect herself. Jimmy had tried. He did his best. For sixteen years he stuck by her. But he had a right to be safe without the dead weight of his mother on his mind. Right now, he balanced a list in his brain.

Money.

Bike.

Reservation.

At the dresser, he tugged at the wooden drawer. Stuck. He tugged again. Stupid drawer. He grabbed the knobs with both hands until the drawer scraped open. Again, the items inside didn't look harassed by strange hands. Cluttered, but not disturbed. Video games, the list, his wallet and the Ute scrapbook.

He'd have to leave the list. He needed to travel light. Besides the trailer wasn't on fire, he could recover it once everyone was safe. He pushed the fear of tribal rejection down into his shoes. He had no choice. He had to run. Pyen would look for him. And as much as she hated the reservation, she would come to him. Right?

Not one moment could be spent on wondering whether his mother loved that devil more than her own son. That kind of thinking would make him hesitate and the white man would win.

With his hand still in the drawer, he fingered his wallet. Out of any camera's view, he could feel the four slips of paper money. More evidence of the deputy's involvement. A real crook or drug addict would have stolen the cash first. Frustration climbed from his heart to warm his face. He had to bite back those emotions in front of the camera. He needed to act normal. Calm. Trusting.

And what was that?

In his drawer, he noticed something new.

A crumpled-up Taco Bell sack.

He dropped the wallet. He had broken his bad habit of eating fast food, but the deputy didn't know that. The demon had never seen the fat Jimmy. Surveillance wouldn't catch the past. Only one person could have left it.

Coyote Joe.

Unbelievable.

His heart beat faster.

Carefully, he went over to the bed and pulled out the plastic grocery sack from the trash can. Back at the dresser, he removed the wadded-up bag and added it to the other random pieces of trash.

If Coyote Joe took the PSP, why not the wallet. Deputy Benson set up everything. But Coyote Joe had gotten the better of the white man and left Jimmy a clue. If the devil had any real police skills, the bag would have intrigued him like an uncooperative witness.

Jimmy couldn't open the contents here and have them confiscated. His fingers trembled. Coyote Joe hadn't let him down. The deputy was a hack. Jimmy needed to remember that.

"You missing anything else?"

Jimmy jumped.

"Did I startle you?" Deputy Benson leaned against the door frame.

Jimmy could have sworn he shut the door. How long had the deputy been standing there watching? He didn't hear the latch click or the hinges squeak. He lowered his arms and let the precious bag of trash dangle at his side. This white man seemed more ghost than human. He didn't resemble Dad. And Jimmy didn't believe in reincarnation, but the hairs rose on his arms all the same.

"Did the guy take anything else?" The deputy asked again.

"No." Jimmy walked back to his dresser and picked up his wallet. "Not even this."

The deputy smiled and scratched his caterpillar mustache. "Lucky you."

Jimmy tucked the wallet into his back pocket and folded his arms. The plastic bag swung from his fingers. Pyen always told him that lies pile on top of each other like dirt on mountains.

Jimmy had no idea how high Deputy Benson climbed every day, but he planned on unearthing the creep.

"Well, if you discover anything else, have your mother give me a call."

"I'm on it." When horses fly.

The deputy hesitated before turning and marching back down the hall.

Jimmy wanted to collapse with relief, but he couldn't. Not until he left the room and went somewhere without the possibility of cameras. After shoving the drawer closed, he patted the wallet in his back pocket then followed the creep into the narrow hall.

The cloudy expression hadn't left Pyen's face.

"I'm going to meet Devin."

"Is it safe?" His mother asked. Hatred expanded his lungs with each inhale as his mother looked to the deputy for approval. Jimmy bit the inside of his lip. The white man had become too important. The devil's break-in-set-up-hero plan had worked. Jimmy needed to unwrap Coyote Joe's present as soon as possible.

"Just one more thing." The deputy approached close enough to tower over him.

Jimmy froze. Freedom lay inches away. A breath separated him from escaping the toxic smell of bad cologne.

"What's in the bag?"

Jimmy turned around as casually as possible. "Trash."

The deputy stretched out his hand. "This is still a crime scene."

Pyen averted her eyes.

Nothing to do but hand it over. Jimmy couldn't hesitate or act suspicious. He watched as the white man spilled all the contents on the table. One by one he examined old school notes and gum wrappers. The Taco Bell bag came out fifth with still a half dozen items remaining.

The deputy rolled the wad around before setting it on the table.

He didn't mean to exhale loud, but he must have because the white man picked up Coyote Joe's secret again. The devil kept his evil eyes on Jimmy while he unwrapped the bag and shook it a couple of times. Jimmy leaned on one leg as if bored and continued the staring contest with the deputy.

When nothing fell out, the deputy dropped it back into the paper bag with the rest.

"What are you looking for?" Pyen asked.

"Nothing in particular." The deputy smiled at her. He ruffled through the trash a little more before handing it back to Jimmy. "We all just need to be careful not to destroy any evidence."

"Can I go now?" You whacked-out worm.

"Of course." The white man leaned back and placed his arm around Pyen.

Jimmy turned and hurried out the door. The sight of that devil's power sent an involuntary tremble through Jimmy's body. He swallowed the yuck in his throat and ran to the dumpster. A couple of gawkers wandered around. With stealth, he removed the Taco Bell sack from the bag and stuffed it in his pocket. The rest he tossed into the trash.

From the corner of his eye, he thought he saw the kitchen curtain move.

CHAPTER 21

Q: *Did dinosaurs live underwater?*
A: *No, other animal types lived underwater. Ripple marks near a*
fossil indicate that those dinosaurs lived near shallow water.

Jimmy constantly checked to make sure the deputy's truck didn't roar up behind him. Or Pyen's stupid Malibu. He needed to be sure he wasn't tracked into the Memorial Park. He stood on his pedals and pumped his way up the short hill. At the flattened top, he made his way to the tall pine tree in the center where he'd first met Devin.

The late afternoon sun cast the shadows away from the base of the tree. The cemetery stretched out like a field rather than a graveyard. Most of the markers lay flat against the fresh mowed grass. Peace wafted across the mountain top in a soft breeze. He dropped his bike on the curb and uncrumpled the wad in his pocket.

The empty paper crinkled.

A crow cawed.

A few dried salsa stains left a peppery smell of what the old man had eaten.

Jimmy laid it flat on his bent knee. And breathed.

The paper wasn't blank. Uneven words covered the page. A note. The creative old Ute warrior had transformed the bag.

Instead of using the sack as wrapping paper for a gift, he pulled apart the glued bottom making it a perfect piece of writing paper. No magic potion. In the scrawled lettering of an old man, Coyote Joe left Jimmy a private message.

He shook both of his hands to relieve his nerves.

Coyote Joe came through.

Before he could read it, the wind lifted the paper from his lap. It floated on a crooked trajectory before it landed upside down on the black pavement. The breeze rolled the bag end over end across the grass. Across the graves. Jimmy had too much respect for the dead to trample over the sleeping, so he pedaled his way around the enclosed patch of lawn. He kept an eye on the paper as it cartwheeled across the silent graves.

By the time he reached the opposite curb, a truck pulled into the cemetery. Jimmy grabbed the bag without getting off his bike. This time he held the letter tight. He was too close to freedom to let go now.

He sat on his bike at the top of the hill holding the note and waiting for the maintenance guy to leave. The small truck drove around the lot before parking near the cemetery house. An old man in a green uniform got out and went into the building.

Jimmy exhaled. He waited to re-opened Coyote Joe's words. He wanted to cherish them. Something about this moment felt pivotal to him. For his entire life, he—like every other kid on the planet—had been stuck in the middle of his mother's life. Her home. Her decisions. What other choice does a child have?

But as a mild wind brushed against him, he spotted the change. The moment when the umbilical cord severed for real. Once he opened this note, he would no longer be Pyen's boy. He would always be her son. Today he would become his own man.

He had to make his own choices. He knew before he read the note from the old homeless Indian that he would follow someone other than his mother. It hit him. It struck him like a blow from his father. Her choices didn't have to be his.

Without waiting for the truck to leave, Jimmy opened the note. Let the maintenance man watch. Who cared? He didn't ride back into the shade of the pine. Trembling and scrambling and hiding were done. Instead he let the high-desert sun bake his back. With a cool sense of satisfaction, he ironed Coyote Joe's letter on his pant leg. A breeze whipped the paper. He faced the sky and grunted.

The wind retreated.

The paper stopped quivering.

Sorry, man, I didn't mean to take your stuff. Life doesn't always give us good choices. I had no choice. I might go to jail. But I still want you to see the rez.

I hid an ancient Nuchu cure in The Monument I want you to get. Just follow the instructions below. Your little friend can help, BUT DON'T let the cops find out. When you're done meet me behind the Walmart, any night around 8:00, I'm always there. Unless I'm in jail, then someone else will be there. They will take you to Bottle Hollow.

Just go to The Monument. Hike thru a trail called "Sound of Silence" . . .

The breeze whipped the paper's edges. The gust smelled free. Like a fresh dose of oxygen mixed with pine and summer. Jimmy scanned the instructions Coyote Joe listed, which included hiking a trail called "Sound of Silence."

Hiking.

His knees felt weak and his stomach hurt. He gripped the handlebars. The paper crumpled between fist and metal. A memory surged against him. A fire pit. He tried to push the word hiking from his brain, but it stuck there, making it hard to breathe. He laid his bike on the pavement and sat down.

"Dad's dead." Jimmy rocked back and forth. "Dad's dead."

He rubbed his thumb against the fingertips on his left hand. The smooth skin didn't have tiny-fingerprint lines.

"Dad's dead."

His wrinkled prints had melted away when Jimmy was five. Back then, Dad forced him to hold a gray ember from the previous night's fire.

"Dad's dead."

A small Jimmy dropped the hot coal three times before he

screamed the numbers one through five.

"Dad's dead." He closed his eyes and repeated the words until the d's and a's and e's blended together on his tongue. They stopped being words and turned into redundant syllables. "Dad's dead. Dads dead. Dadsdead. Dadsdeaddadsdead."

He forced a hard exhale. Coyote Joe didn't know James Maxwell Hunter. The old man wouldn't set him up. No one would be on the hike to force Jimmy to do anything he didn't want to do. He stopped rocking and took in a dozen heavy breaths.

"Dad's dead." This time the words came out calm and confident. Jimmy found himself chanting the mantra twice within one day. The deputy triggered things in his heart best left alone. No doubt there'd be more memories stirred up in the days and months to come.

"You okay?"

He opened his eyes.

The old maintenance man stood before him. "You look lost." His white face wrinkled from sun and age. He looked familiar, but all old white men have the same bland features. Jimmy straightened his back. He didn't need to answer.

"Maybe you lost something then." The white man held Coyote Joe's note in his hand. At some point in his PTSD he'd let go of the Taco Bell paper. The old guy glanced at it once more before handing it back to Jimmy. "Need to be careful about things like this."

Discomfort settled around Jimmy's heart. What did the man know? Was he a spy? The town of Vernal stretched out below them. Across the hills to the west, the reservation spread miles wide. As the man hobbled away, Jimmy relaxed his shoulders. Whatever. Let the spy tell the deputy. Jimmy was too close to freedom to care. This time when he shook out the paper to read it, he kept his grip tight. He had to be careful. He couldn't slip up. A billion things would try to get in the way of his success and he had to avoid them.

Many of the instructions didn't make any sense. Coyote Joe mentioned "The Monument." The only monuments he'd ever seen were in Washington D.C. And he couldn't remember any stone statues around Vernal. Unless he considered the dinosaur replicas.

Maybe Coyote Joe meant the Big Pink dinosaur on Highway 40 that looked like a gigantic, happy-meal toy. Or the big T. rex the town dressed up in costumes near Taco Bell. Maybe all the life-size dinosaurs in the museum on Main Street were called "The Monument."

Jimmy had no idea. But Devin would. Problem was people—especially white people— couldn't be trusted. Yet the very edge of the reservation lingered and he couldn't do it alone. Could he? Maybe Devin wasn't an obstacle to be avoided.

He stuffed the note from Coyote Joe into his pocket and pedaled around the center plot in the cemetery. He could ask around. But the deputy might find out. He could google it. But that might take forever. Not the kind of time he had available.

After his seventh or eighth lap. He stopped under the tree where he first met Devin. It was a risk. A big one. But the result of not calling would weigh more. With a deep sigh, he pulled out his cell phone and called.

Within minutes, Devin cleared up many of the questions in the note.

"First of all, the Monument isn't a statue."

"It's not?"

"It's like a national park. A huge section of land the government owns and protects."

"From what?" Jimmy didn't like the implication.

"I don't know, people."

"So, we can't go there?"

"We can."

"I don't get it." Jimmy didn't mean to raise his voice, but Devin needed to get to the point. Government land or not, Jimmy had to go. His entire future rested in this one crumpled piece of paper. This crinkled ray of hope.

"The land's protected. You know, for hiking and camping and stuff."

"Oh, is that all? Then let's go."

"Didn't you hear me say it's protected?"

"So?"

"You can go into a national monument, but you can't dig up buried treasure."

"Says who? Look, all of this land used to belong to my ancestors, and if there's some kind of root or plant or stone Coyote Joe knows about that will give me access to the reservation, then as a Ute, I have more right to it than the government."

"And what if we're caught?"

Jimmy didn't answer right away. He wiped the sweat from his palms on his pants and waited. He didn't have all the answers, some of them would have to be figured out along the way. Like this one, "We'll go at night."

"Excuse me?"

"You said this monument place is near the quarry."

"Right."

"And your Gram lives close enough for us to get there by bike."

"So."

"We will camp in your front yard then sneak away at dark. We'd be back before morning."

"Absolutely not. I refuse to lie to Gram and Gramps."

"Right." The word came with one loud laugh. One thing everyone knows, kids lie to their parents all the time. Not only that, there was an excitement in knowing that what they were about to do was against the law.

"I don't lie."

Jimmy bit back his frustration. He couldn't risk losing Devin and his knowledge and his help. Unless he just went ahead and went to the reservation by himself. He still had that option. It was still a good idea. He didn't like begging this kid for anything. And he especially didn't want to owe him.

The sun stretched itself toward the western horizon. If he was going to head to the reservation today, he needed to do it before he lost daylight. He'd give the kid one more shot and if he couldn't motivate him, then he'd hang up and go ahead and start biking his way to the reservation. "It's for my mother." He cleared his throat to dispel the strain that lodged itself there. "It's up to you." Those words came out harder and more clear.

Devin exhaled. "Let me think about it."

"Never mind." Jimmy rested the phone on his shoulder and kicked the pedal.

"I didn't say no, but this whole plan is crazy. You don't know anything about this Coyote Joe person. This could be a set-up. He could be trying to trap us there so he can kidnap us or something."

"Why, because that's what Indians do?"

"Nobody's talking about Indians, I'm talking about criminals."

"If he wanted to hurt me, he'd have done it already." Jimmy recounted what the Vernal City cop said about Deputy Benson. "How shady does a cop have to be for other cops to not trust him? I've got to do this. Pyen is in serious danger. It's one night, one dig. We're in and we're out. I could be one-hundred percent wrong, and if I am, I'll give it all up. But what if I'm right? What if that whack-job becomes my dad and my mother pays for it with her life?"

"But how do you know Coyote Joe's not crazy."

"I'm not asking you to trust Coyote Joe, I'm asking you to trust me."

Devin exhaled. Jimmy could tell the kid was scared, but he could also tell he was changing his mind. He leaned back his head and smiled to the sky, Plan A had just become Plan B.

CHAPTER 22

Q: *Where have dinosaur fossils been found?*
A: *On every continent on Earth.*

For the next week, Jimmy and Devin made plans. Jimmy's heart still desperately wanted to get to the reservation, but Coyote Joe had provided him with a better way to do it. He wasn't giving up on the idea, he was enhancing it. At least he kept telling himself that's what he was doing. He refused to let his brain rest on the idea that he might be afraid to go. That just couldn't be true. Every time a thought crawled into his head that maybe Pyen had good reasons to not return, Jimmy swatted them away.

The reservation would prove her wrong. It had to, because if it didn't, that meant this sucky life would always be sucky. And Jimmy couldn't go there. Instead he made new lists with Devin of what they needed.

The tent.

Camping equipment.

A map.

Devin's Gram had agreed. Everything was set, except, permission from Pyen. He'd get that tonight. He'd been trying to ask her for days, but he could never get her alone. The deputy had dinner with them every night. The devil took her on errands. His control of their daily tasks grew exponentially.

Devin set the date for the second-to-last Friday night in June. Two days away. If Jimmy didn't talk to her now, he would be forced to sneak out that night. If she caught him, she'd tell the deputy and that can of worms needed to stay closed as long as possible.

Besides, he wasn't going to tell her all the details. Just enough for a yes. So, as Pyen cleared the dishes, Deputy Benson moved to the couch to watch NASCAR on cable. Something he paid for. Jimmy carried the dirty plates to the sink. He introduced the topic after he asked about her work. The conversation started off quiet enough, until Pyen lifted her voice and said, "I don't know, Paa."

"Not so loud," He whispered to her and glanced over at the white man. No movement to join them yet. "Let's talk outside."

"No. I want to finish these."

"It's important." He gritted his teeth. "What's the big deal? I'm not asking to go to the moon."

"I don't like the idea of you camping out at night."

"Listen to your mother." The deputy spoke up from the couch without taking his ugly eyes off the television.

"Pyen," Jimmy sneered at his mother. He meant it for the deputy, but she'd do. The demon wouldn't show any real violence this early in the relationship. And if he did, Jimmy would win anyway. No point whispering anymore. "We'll be in Devin's front yard. His Gram and Gramps will be in the house less than fifty feet away."

"There's just so much trouble around these days."

He nodded and intentionally looked over at the deputy. Pyen went back to the sink. Coward. She knew what he meant. She had to know. He paced the small kitchen. "So, I'm never going to be able to spend time with my friends? School's out and I want to find a job next month. Come on. What more do you want from me?"

This was all Pyen's fault. All of it. From the beginning to the end. She'd never done anything to escape the beast, and now she wanted to drag Jimmy right back into the private, violent life of a white man. What made him think she'd become a better ally now. She hadn't so far. "I'm going to go."

"Watch the way you speak to your mother, son."

"I'm not your son. Got that?" He glared at the man.

The deputy set the remote on the coffee table and turned toward them. Jimmy faced Pyen. "It's because of him, right? It's because you think this man has all the answers for this family. Well. He doesn't."

"Jimmy, don't go there. Don't say stuff like that. Andrew is important to me."

"I can see that."

"You don't need to be jealous of our relationship." The deputy stood up.

"I'm not jealous!" Jimmy eyed the man from his hat hair to his square cop shoes. "What kind of twisted mess is that? You don't know anything about me or my mother to say something like that."

"Jimmy." His mother pleaded.

"Don't beg, Pyen. Don't." He hated how this white man had transformed his mother back into a groveling idiot. "Never mind, it was just for one night. I'll call Devin and tell him no."

"I didn't say that." Pyen bit her lip. She flitted her fingers toward them both. "Give me a minute, I need to think."

The deputy approached her and coiled his arms around her. "Of course." He patted Pyen's back. "This is a decision between you and your son."

He kissed her cheek, put on his wide-brimmed deputy hat and walked out the door. Anger had to be building up underneath that pasty skin.

White men were crazy. Jimmy didn't want to choose between the reservation and Pyen, but he couldn't go back to his former life. He never wanted it that way. But Pyen had made her intentions clear. She'd never would take him to the tribe. With two full years before graduation, he couldn't wait that long.

"Look, you have your friends and I have mine." He straightened his back, making him another inch taller. "Don't fight me on this." His stomach turned. He knew those words. He knew their tone. The voice of his father penetrated the grave and escaped his mouth. The same calm with threatening undertones.

And as much as he wanted to grab the words from the air and tuck them back inside of him, he wouldn't because it worked. Her muscles tightened at the throat. Her shoulders tensed and she said, "Okay."

"Good."

But when he went to his room, he felt like he lost ground with her instead of gaining it. Nothing good about it.

CHAPTER 23

Q: Did dinosaurs grieve?
A: Evidence of animals reacting to death or
loss has been documented. However, reptiles
aren't as likely to require social relationships.

The sun cast the last of its orange glow against the sheer cliff of Split Mountain, east of Devin's front yard. Jimmy was on Devin's turf. The boy's Gram's house sat on the highway leading to Dinosaur National Monument. Devin was supposed to introduce them on the day of the quarry date, but that didn't happen.

Today, the two old white people were part of the process. He patted the back pocket of his jeans. Coyote Joe's folded instructions made a thick, wallet-sized wad. Before the sunrise, he would have what he needed to enter the reservation and stay.

"That's my Gram." Devin pointed toward the white paneled house.

Jimmy squinted. Not because he couldn't see, more because he couldn't believe what he saw. The white-haired lady with the cane that motioned them over looked like the woman from the quarry bus.

He flipped his braid over his shoulder and followed Devin to the porch.

"Hey, Charlie, come see." She shouted before they reached the steps. "It's the nice boy from the quarry. You know the one who gave the tourist girl a bracelet."

"What is she talking about?" Devin asked.

"Nothing." Jimmy kept walking. The Uintah Basin suddenly felt small and tight.

The old man who appeared confirmed it. They were at the quarry the same day as the date. More than that. Devin's Gramp was the maintenance man at the cemetery. The man who rescued Coyote Joe's note from the wind. He nodded when Devin introduced them but didn't smile.

The coincidences were starting to pile up. Did this old man know the deputy?

"You boys need some help with your tent?" Devin's Gram asked. Based on her health, she obviously offered her husband's services, not her own.

"No," Devin answered. "We're good."

"What are you doing out there tonight?" Suspicion laced the old man's voice. A white man's voice, aged but still there. The tone of control and want for power. "What are your plans?"

Devin shrugged "Smoke some crack. You know, the usual."

The old lady laughed while the man squinted and tipped his head. "Very funny." He didn't laugh. Instead he just kept looking at Jimmy. He looked long enough for Jimmy to wonder if the old man had read the note before handing it back to Jimmy that day.

"My friend's never been camping, so I'm showing him the ropes."

"Aww. That's nice for our Devin to let you try it." His Gram said.

"Yes, ma'am." Jimmy answered.

The white man stood with his arms folded across his chest. Jimmy resisted giving Devin a good shove for making a joke of it. For raising suspicion. For talking at all. But in the end, the old man just said, "Nice to meet you." And went back inside.

As they headed back to the pile of tent supplies, Jimmy fumed. The last thing he needed was another white man on his case, especially one who might rat them out to the deputy. He shook the tent tarp out like a bed sheet. "Are you trying to get us caught?" He whispered.

"Yup." Devin pulled the stakes from a bag. "I think we should take Gramps with us."

"Are you nuts?" Jimmy glanced back at Devin. He wasn't joking. What a coward. Back at the house, Devin's Gramps no longer stood on the porch, but Jimmy still felt the old man's presence. From the backyard, the smell of burning charcoal wafted into the air and smoke tickled the evening sky. His stomach nagged him. "No one can come."

As if on cue, Devin's younger brother ran over to them. "Can I help?"

"No!" Jimmy said at the same time Devin said, "Sure!"

The little kid glared at Jimmy. The boy could only be six or seven. "He's too young."

"I'm ten."

"No way. Does everyone in your family look like babies?"

Devin glared at him. "One day, you might just be lucky enough to meet my older brother."

"Yeah," the little brat poked out his lip. "He'd beat you up fast."

"Whatever. We don't need this crap."

"You used a bad word and I'm telling Gram." The miniature Devin ran away and Jimmy didn't care. Couldn't care. He needed to validate Devin's commitment.

"If you don't want to go, then let's cancel it. All of it."

"I didn't say that."

"Then quit trying to invite everyone into our conversation."

A prairie dog dashed into sagebrush as a Jeep rumbled up the highway toward the Monument. The vehicle pulled a trailer with a couple of four-wheelers on it. Jimmy hoped the Monument would be empty. He turned to Devin. "I think you're chicken."

"No, I'm not." Devin flinched as a red-tailed hawk screamed across the sky.

"Stop acting like it." Jimmy hadn't felt this free since fourth grade when his father left for Afghanistan. No jet fuel in the air tonight, only the lingering smoke of charcoal and wood.

James Maxwell Hunter had insisted his son be a "big boy" and not cry. Not a problem. He wanted his father to go. It meant he could relax. It meant he could sleep. It meant the US military would eliminate terrorism from his house.

"You don't have to act so tough." Devin snapped his end of the flexible black rod to the top of the tent.

Jimmy ignored him. The three-man tent arched like a cat from a nap. The metal end of the pole slipped into a matching hole. With a hammer, he cracked the muddy clay earth. He hated when his mind went back. He adjusted the post in the ground and smacked the head hard and it sank deep, securing the tent to the ground. He hated how fresh the memories felt. Fear. Panic. Tears. He wiped his nose on his sleeve before Devin could see. It was stupid to get anxious — they would camp in the front yard, far from the burning coals.

From opposite sides the sound of hammer against spikes reminded Jimmy that he wasn't alone. He wasn't five and he needed to make sure Devin didn't change his mind. With the four sides completed, they dusted off their jeans.

Jimmy grabbed the two sleeping bags and tossed one to Devin. He had to draw the boy a little deeper into his past, secure the night's adventure.

They climbed into the tent. Without the light from the porch or the fading sun, shadows accompanied the rustle of fabric. He figured out what he could reveal to this kid. He wasn't worried. Devin practically knew everything already. A little more wouldn't hurt. "Have you ever seen a dead person?"

"No."

"I checked my dad's casket." He unrolled his bag.

"You did?" Devin sounded impressed.

"I had to." Jimmy tucked his long legs under him. A couple strands came loose from his braid, so he tucked them behind his ear. "What if they made a mistake? What if the monster wasn't really dead?"

"What did he look like?"

"Empty." He closed his eyes. This was it. The boy would either trust him or laugh at him. Risk verses results. With his eyes still closed, he said, "the beast lay there stiff and gray in his uniform." Jimmy opened his eyes. "For the first time my father's power left him. His body looked lifeless, like a snail shell. But back then I was still so afraid of him, even dead. During the entire funeral," he squeezed his hands together into one fist. "I waited for him to sit up. And made plans to grab my mother's hand and run."

"Wow."

"But that didn't happen." He remembered how different oxygen tasted after the casket lid closed and the last shovel of dirt buried the beast. He took in a fresh breath now and felt the same delicious taste of freedom. The night air entered his lungs with the same power as it had the night he broke the window to escape the fire. "Things are very different now, though."

CHAPTER 24

Q: *How long did dinosaurs live?*
A: *Most dinosaurs probably lived fifty to sixty years.*

The smell of campfires and barbeque remained in the air as the clouds darkened the summer sky. "Looks like rain."

Devin's Gramps studied the sky as he carried in the last of the condiments into the house. "I'd hate to be caught in the Monument tonight in a microburst."

Jimmy froze. Why had the old man mentioned the Monument? There was still the very real possibility that the old man had read the note back at the cemetery. Devin's Gram carefully climbed the steps back into the house. This old woman wouldn't let them camp out if she knew they had plans to escape. No. He was just being paranoid.

"The weatherman predicted a summer storm. If the rain becomes too much—" the old woman stopped in the doorway and messed up Devin's hair "— you boys come in okay?"

"We'll be fine," Devin answered. Jimmy nodded a thanks and walked around the house to where they'd pitched their tent. If the old man knew, then he knew. Nothing Jimmy could do about it. They had seven hours to get into the Monument and out again. If he had to do it alone, he'd try. Nothing could stop him now that he was this close. Not the old man and certainly not the rain. Besides, in the couple months Jimmy'd been in Vernal, it hadn't rained once. Too much virga. Far as he was concerned, the cloud-filled sky provided cover. They had planned to leave at midnight, but now the evening was dark enough to slip out early.

Devin caught up with him. "Rain in the desert isn't good."

"Don't tell me you're afraid of thunder."

"Don't be dumb."

They climbed into the tent.

"Rain in those canyons causes flash floods."

"We can't stop now."

"You really don't care if you live or die, do you?"

Jimmy couldn't believe what the kid was saying. "Of course, I do. Why do you think I'm doing this?"

He began to stuff their supplies into his backpack. Jimmy might be a lot of things, but suicidal wasn't one of them. "'Every day's a struggle of life and death for me. Every day."

It wasn't Devin's fault he had no idea the rain was nothing compared to the danger waiting for Jimmy back in town. He wished he could do this alone. He wished he didn't need this kid. But some things couldn't be helped. He knew nothing of the area, the Monument or the trails. He needed this kid and they were going. With a hand on Devin's shoulder he reassured him, "We'll be fine."

Devin didn't look convinced, but he got his stuff ready anyway.

They snuck down to the creek where they'd hidden their bikes. A three-mile ride took them down invisible roads through the sleeping neighborhood of Jensen. The illumination of a lamppost cast a glow across the entrance to Dinosaur National Monument.

Utah Highway 149 curved around the banks of the Green River, not that he could see it. But the flow of water wrestled over rocks to his right. Crickets stopped complaining as he and Devin pedaled past shadows along the highway. Around the open bend ahead, two white headlights weaved in their direction. With mountains piled to the left and the river on the right, soon Jimmy and Devin would be spotlighted in the driver's beams.

Jimmy stopped his bike. The kid's eyes widened. Dinosaur-sized trouble waited for them at home if either one of them got caught.

"Quick, down here." Devin dropped into the thick brush. They laid their bikes down first then sunk as flat to the ground as possible. The tang of sage and dirt choked the air. They had a handful of yards between human eyes and a flowing river. Getting wet would be better than being seen.

The rumble of a truck engine drew close like a sniffing hound. Most drivers sped through the 45 MPH zone. This guy didn't top 25. Jimmy held his breath even though the driver couldn't possibly hear him over the twangy sounds of Eagle Country 105.5.

The rub of tires against pavement passed over his head. He ducked low enough to taste dirt. The bright white of headlights illuminated the brush and moved on. In a minute, they'd be up on their bikes and back on track.

That's what Jimmy thought, until Devin started kicking and screaming. "Ants."

"Shh," Jimmy reached over to cover Devin's mouth. The boy could ruin everything because of some dumb— "Owwww." The sting on his ankles felt like fire. These crazy ants stung like bees. He patted his legs and wanted to cry.

Bright red taillights shined above them.

Oh, crap.

The truck's brakes whined.

He heard Devin splash into the river and Jimmy placed his burning leg in as well. The water was icy but one hundred times better than horrible sting from what Devin called ants. He stood as the water pushed gently around his legs. This night was theirs to win or lose, and losing wasn't an option.

The country music ended.

The air grew silent.

Even the crickets waited to see if the driver would exit his car to search.

The river continued its steady flow.

Devin squirmed out of it before standing still. Jimmy didn't care as long as Devin remained quiet. Angry adults waited for both of them back home. And Jimmy wondered if the man who drove the truck might not be worse. He could be a poacher, armed and ready to steal more than rabbits in a protected area. A gun in the hand of a white man made his head ache. Maybe he'd be killed by the enemy regardless of his plans. He pushed back the terror rising inside of him and pressed down harder against the river bank to steady the chill sweeping over his legs.

A whiff of Old Spice sent prickles across his skin. What are the chances? No Way. Demon Benson couldn't have known about the trip. Then a million reasons why the deputy would know entered Jimmy's mind. But he had to push them away. He couldn't let paranoia overcome him. Maybe Old Spice was the only cologne available in Vernal.

That was it.

Then Jimmy heard the man's cell ring.

"Hello," the voice of Deputy Benson answered the phone from the shadows above them.

Jimmy froze like a frightened deer. How had this crazy stalker trailed them? The note hadn't left his pocket. He never opened it where cameras could see. The power of this man blanketed the situation in failure. The adventure was spinning out of control. Neither Jimmy nor Devin could save this day — or any other day.

The river pulled water unwillingly south. If the deputy came near them, he would jump right into the river and let the current take him where it wanted.

"On my way."

The brake lights evaporated.

Exhaust fumes penetrated the sage.

Jimmy didn't move. He stayed in position as the sound of the river's current eventually became the only sound left to hear. The truck was gone, but Jimmy continued to tremble at how close they'd come to being caught.

"I'm going home." Devin climbed away from the river.

Jimmy didn't respond. His breaths came out in puffs. Bits of the world came to him but from a distance. Devin saying something about, "No more secrets. No more ants. No more almost dying in the river." But the words were only vapors to Jimmy that floated up into the sky. Overpowered by the presence of his own truth.

Deputy Benson was formidable. Maybe too formidable. Until this moment Jimmy never really understood why people were so freaked out about stalkers. But crap, the appearance of the demon messed with Jimmy's head. A punch he could take. A slap. A stab. But this guy, he's like a frickin' ghost.

"Jimmy."

He didn't answer. It didn't matter. He couldn't beat a ghost. He couldn't.

"Jimmy." Devin's voice got louder.

He looked at the shadow of the boy who almost got caught with him. His face dark and impossible to see in the cloud-covered night. Ghost meat, that's what they'd almost been.

"Jimmy, get out of the water before you drown."

He complied. Why not? Seemed like a reasonable request. Except the part about drowning in knee-deep water. Devin helped him carry his bike to the road. The boy wanted to go back. To be honest, so did Jimmy.

The burning in his ankles returned as his legs began to warm up.

"I'm going back."

"I know." Jimmy nodded his head. He pointed his bike toward the Monument. "Thanks for bringing me this far."

Devin stopped and hung his head. "Why are you so stubborn?"

"Me? Why am I so stubborn? Why don't you ask that to the crazy deputy who's stalking us?" He reached down and furiously rubbed the ant stings on his ankles, wishing he could plunge the burning bites back into the cool Green River.

"Seriously?" Devin rubbed his ankles too. "That was the deputy?"

"Yeah."

"That's bad. The deputy has no reason to be in the Monument. Rangers patrol this area, not deputies." The kid stopped rubbing. "Only one thing could have him driving around. He knows our plans. What if he stops by Gram's?"

"I don't care." Jimmy bounced his front tire against the asphalt. He couldn't care. "What's the difference? If we're caught, we're caught."

"No, I have to go back." Devin pointed his bike away from the Monument.

"I said go, didn't I?" They were wasting time. Jimmy didn't know where this stupid trail was, but the kid wanted to go, then he should go. Jimmy'd find what he needed alone, if necessary. Nothing but trouble waited for him if he went back.

In the dark, Jimmy couldn't see the disappointment on Devin's face, but he could hear it in his voice. "He could be at my Gram's right now."

"Then we're already in trouble, right? Might as well continue. Look," he palmed the handlebars to avoid rubbing the handful of burns just above his socks, "if we turn back, I'll never get another chance to be free. This note is my only hope. You and this note."

Devin sighed. Jimmy started to pedal forward. The kid was the first person he'd trusted since he was five years old. This was the kid's moment of truth. A chance for him to decide and for Jimmy to discover if the kid had any metal. Either way, Jimmy's destiny lay in Dinosaur National Monument.

CHAPTER 25

Q: *Did dinosaurs ever fight each other?*
A: *Fossils show evidence of teeth marks and fractures in bones indicating a real battle to survive.*

The black landscape provided only a few feet of visibility. The clouds hid more than the moon, they hid areas where the road turned. They hid a small booth where people paid to enter the protected land. Jimmy didn't see it until they were right up on it. He was one-hundred percent dependent on Devin. One-hundred percent trusting. It was hard, but Jimmy had to acknowledge the kid was acting like a real friend.

Jimmy wrestled with that idea as he followed the kid deeper into the Monument without a word. He'd never had a friend like this before. Not someone who risked trouble for him. Not someone he allowed in. But it was done and there was nothing to do but continue.

Jimmy never actually thought this adventure would be easy. Maybe he just didn't expect the obstacles so early. First Devin's Gramp might know. Then the deputy's appearance. And now the continued but slowly fading burn of bites on his ankles. His nerves were fried by the time Devin stopped and said, "This is it."

There wasn't anything to see. Just a black expanse of

nothingness, similar to the vast expanse of nothingness that surrounded them all the way. Devin took out his flashlight and Jimmy could read the sign "Sound of Silence Trail."

"Great." He got off his bike wishing the clouds would part so the moon could help them out a little. He took a sip from one of the two bottles of water he had and grabbed his flashlight as well. It didn't illuminate much further than a few feet, but far enough to reveal a trench between them and the path.

"How are we supposed to get past that?" Jimmy asked. He didn't want to leave their bikes on the road in case the deputy returned.

"We'll have to carry them to the wash."

Devin went first with his bike over his head and Jimmy followed with his flashlight gripped in his teeth. The low sage cast shifting shadows as the wind pushed against them. The adventure had begun, almost like a contest between them and Deputy Benson. The white man showed his intent to win by extending his surveillance into shadowing them. If he wanted a contest, there would be one winner and one loser. And Jimmy had to win.

He rolled his bike far enough to not create any reflection from passing cars. A spotlight would still find them, the adjustable kind screwed to the side of cop cars.

"Get some brush."

"No. Our tires are messing with the soil."

"Soil?" Jimmy gasped.

"Seriously. It's microbiotic and fragile." Devin's flashlight spanned across the ground and he took extra care to keep his bike on the trail.

"We can't take them the whole way."

"No, we'll leave them in the wash."

"Whatever." He didn't have time to worry about microbiotic soil, but he owed Devin something for still being here. It was very possible that the boy would get a lashing from that grandfather of his when they got back. No one had ever gone this far out on a limb for him before, and Jimmy respected that.

He tried not to think of the deputy pulling up in front of Devin's house. Each step on the trail could be mirrored by the white devil. Any moment now, the white man could be lifting the flap on their abandoned tent. Hopefully the recorded sound of snoring from Jimmy's cell phone would trick them all. It sounded corny, but who cared. Hopefully no one would come out to the tent to check. Devin kept his phone to use some "geocaching GPS" app that Jimmy'd never heard of.

Thoughts of getting lost or caught had to be tossed aside. He had to trust his plan. One minute spent on the deputy's game would be a distraction. All his instincts about the man let him know enough. Forward was the only way to go. He had no choice but to get to the treasure Coyote Joe buried and bring it to Walmart. Proof that he deserved an audience with the tribal elders.

About a hundred yards from the entrance they stepped off the soft sand and down into the rocky wash. They dumped their bikes. The lighter load had him hustling behind the bouncing glow of his flashlight. They were doing it. He slowed down and scanned the elevated bank. His heart raced with relief. They were here. If there had been any doubt hiding in the back of his soul, it was gone now. All the obstacles had been surpassed. He scanned the area again, wanting to capture as much as possible knowing this moment would be his to own forever. His flashlight reflected off a white porcelain skull. He scrambled toward it.

"What are you doing?" Devin hurried to catch up.

"It's a sign. A trophy."

"You really are nuts."

"Why? Because I understand the importance of what I'm doing?"

"And I don't?"

"Nobody said that." He stuffed the skull into his backpack and stomped back onto the trail.

"Dead things carry diseases, you know." Devin hollered at him.

"Not when the meat's gone." He shouted back. His voice echoed against the flat surface of a stone mountain. They couldn't keep shouting and expect to continue to stay ahead of the deputy. He slowed down and waited for his friend. "At least we don't have to worry about rattlesnakes."

"What are you talking about?"

"Snakes don't come out at night."

"Who told you that?"

Dinosaurs were the only animals Jimmy had ever studied. He'd made the comment because it only made sense.

"Trust me." Devin waved his flashlight along the trail in front of him. "All the animals that live in this area are awake."

What a buzz kill. Jimmy wanted to enjoy the rest of the trip, but Devin was proving to be more annoying than helpful. "Okay, besides snakes, what are we talking about? Deer?" Please say, yes.

"Yeah, deer and rabbits, if you're worried about that."

"Not especially." Well, only a little.

"What about bobcats and mountain lions?"

The dark wilderness felt heavy around him. For the first time in his life, the danger of white men dimmed. Claws. Teeth. Horns. Jimmy moved forward making sure to use his flashlight more diligently. "You're full of it." He said with more hope than certainty.

"No, I'm not. This is their home and we're invading it. They know it better than we do. They can smell us. Expect them to protect their space, and you might think deer are sweet and gentle, but trust me, you mess with a herd of them, and they can do some serious damage."

"Are you done?" Jimmy shone his light right in Devin's eyes.

The boy shrugged.

He turned and continued to march on. Like it or not, they were here and they would have to deal with whatever came their way. This trip trumped animal fears. Although Devin didn't mention bears, Jimmy felt ready to fight a grizzly. He was sure of it. Until a half mile later when his flashlight bounced off a pair of bright red eyes in the brush beside them.

CHAPTER 26

Q: What would scare a dinosaur?
A: All animals fear injury. Other animals could
frighten dinosaurs, including bigger dinosaurs.

Jimmy panned his flashlight across the bush.

All the bravado he felt a moment ago vanished into the dark sky.

The eyes in the sage stared at him unblinking. Shadows masked the rest of the creature. Based on height, it could be a rabbit, but the creature didn't run. Hopefully not a crouching bobcat.

Claws pawed at the ground.

Blood whooshed through his ears.

The animal stomped.

He couldn't move

The animal hissed.

He wanted to run, but honestly couldn't.

Maybe it wasn't an animal at all. A crazy idea came to him, maybe the deputy morphed into a supernatural being. Some hideous form of his true self. He'd read books about demons.

"Ridiculous," Jimmy said aloud.

"What's the problem?" Devin scrambled up behind him.

The bright red eyes disappeared.

Devin stopped.

The hissing and scratching ended.

Jimmy leaned forward and pointed the flashlight into the bush.

A furry, white bottom appeared in the light. Musk shot through the beam. He squeezed his face and pulled away from the blast.

Too late.

Oily goop sizzled into his forehead. The smell of rotten eggs cooked over a fire of burning rubber shut down every other sensation in his body. He gagged and coughed as he tried to wipe the goop off. A dry heave forced itself against his throat.

Eyes squeezed tight, he stumbled away, trying to escape the suffocating poison. But puke clung to him.

He didn't want to open his eyes in case the stinky crud leaked down his face.

He wiped his shirt against his face.

The goop smeared.

Probably for the same reason a dog or cat rolled in the dirt, he shoved his face and hands into the dry wash sand and bathed in it. He rolled around more like a pig than a house pet.

"Take off your shirt." Devin's shout sounded twenty feet away.

He immediately complied. Using the part of the fabric that felt dry, he scrubbed his face, especially near his eyes. Then tossed the shirt as far away from him as possible.

"Here let me help." Devin's voice came closer.

Jimmy wanted to swear. Wanted to use every word he'd ever heard his father spout, but he'd never give the skunk gunk a single chance to pass his lips. He felt Devin's hand on the back of his head and a splash of cold water glugged down his face.

Clean and cold, he rubbed the water against his skin until Devin emptied his whole canteen.

"More," Jimmy shouted.

"That's all I have."

"Where's mine?"

"What if we need it for later?"

"What later? We need it now."

Devin shouted "no" and ran from him.

He wiped and wiped all remaining drops from around his face, neck and shoulders. Let Devin keep the water. The smell didn't subside as much as he sensed his nostrils had given up detecting it. He prepared for everything the night could throw at him, except this.

He'd been ready to march back into the daylight with animal scratches and broken skin. He'd even thought it would be heroic to approach the tribe with his arm in a sling.

Signs of a hard victory won.

A true warrior.

Proof of his ability to tame nature.

Instead, a face full of humiliation from the white butt of a skunk. They'd laugh. Of course, they would. They might even kick him out of the reservation before he could plead his case.

CHAPTER 27

Q: *Could a dinosaur fart kill you?*
A: *Any flatulence contains gas, but there's
no evidence of the fumes being poisonous.*

"It shot out of his butt like pee." Devin doubled over in laughter.

Jimmy tried to ignore his friend who now wore his shirt over his nose.

But Devin kept going. "You should have seen it. Like a super soaker. Dude."

He hurried forward. He didn't come here for this. The flashlight beam bounced against the stupid desert shrubs.

Devin chuckled behind him. "Don't be mad at me."

"I'm not mad!" Everything didn't need to be a joke. The skunk spray stung. And not just on his skin, his heart felt heavier. Good thing no one witnessed it besides this idiot. He shivered and rubbed his arms free of prickles.

Devin had offered to give Jimmy his jacket. But even with the evening chill, Jimmy liked having his chest bare. It felt right. Felt native. A real journey to manhood in spite of the humiliation.

"Look on the bright side, there's not an animal in this wilderness that's going to want to come within biting distance now."

"Happy to help." Jimmy gritted his teeth. Okay. Last obstacle conquered. The humiliation was only witnessed by one jerk and he'd never tell because it would get him in trouble. And as they continued to weave through the dark wash, the smell either faded or Jimmy got used to it and his heart lightened. Especially when his flashlight's beam caught the reflective trail markers.

They'd already reached number six. More than half way to ten, the magic number in Coyote Joe's note. A smile crept across Jimmy's face. The sense of accomplishment returned.

A thin trail led up and out of the wash. Jimmy climbed. The sand under his feet became hard. He could move faster through the dry brush than he did on the sand and rocks below. A thin branch scratched his bare skin. The sting of broken flesh provided him a trophy. Better than the skunk attack.

He jumped down to a rock as the mountain gapped.

"The trail goes up." Devin corrected him.

"How do you know?" He was growing resentful of Devin.

"I've taken it before."

Devin climbed like a lizard above him and proceeded down the dark narrow trail.

Whatever.

He put his flashlight in his mouth and climbed back up the confusing trail. For a moment he'd wished he'd come alone. Except this would have been the moment when he'd gotten lost. He might have found the rest of the trail, but it would have been harder without Devin.

Maybe even impossible.

Jimmy somehow missed trail markers seven, eight and nine, but Devin claimed they existed along the small ledge they followed. It carefully took them back down into the wash. A rumble spoke from the clouds. The small rustling of grass at the edge of the wash interrupted the mostly silent canyon. They had to have gone at least a mile before trail marker number ten glowed from the pole in front of them.

"This is it!" He wanted to hug the marker but didn't.

"What?"

"Coyote Joe's note puts the treasure on the other side of this marker."

"We can't go that way."

"Why not?"

"The guide says turn right."

"We're not here to follow the stupid guide." A crash of thunder emphasized the statement.

Devin pointed his flashlight to the sky. "I don't like this."

"So, you've said." Jimmy would welcome the rain. Buckets of cool water cleansing his soul. The shower could erase the skunk and the heaviness. Having Paa as a nickname connected him to water. He'd loved nothing more than the feel and smell of rain. He scanned his flashlight across the dark rock. Sage and juniper limbs reached out, hungry for moisture.

"It's just that a flash flood could kill us."

This time he aimed his flashlight into Devin's squinting face. The white boy didn't know Jimmy's connection to water. Paa was more than a nickname. It fit him. For as long as he could remember, he had the ability to swim like a fish. Rain, showers, rivers, water, were connected to him in ways only an Indian would understand. "We're too big to worry about a little water."

"I've seen huge boulders loosen."

He sighed. "If it starts to rain, we'll get out of the wash. Okay?"

Devin grunted.

"Besides, we heard thunder, but we didn't see any lightning. The storm isn't anywhere near here."

Devin looked up to the sky. "Fine. But let's hurry."

They lumbered over a fallen tree, obviously placed there to keep hikers on track. Unseen clouds blocked the moon and stars from view, but it'd been that way all night. The whole trip had been made with the dim glow of flashlight beams.

"One." Jimmy counted his steps. "Two."

"What are you doing?"

"Counting." He stopped. He didn't want to move and lose track of the number. "Did you even read the note?"

Devin shrugged.

Jimmy didn't need the boy to know. He remembered every

word. Together they counted their paces. After fifty steps, he panned the landscape with light. "There." Like a trapped animal in headlights, they'd spotted the first dead tree. Although it rested more ahead of them than on the right, Coyote Joe's feet were bigger than theirs.

The gnarled branches awakened joy in him. They were close. While living trees never posed the same danger as beasts. He drew comfort from the stiff carcass. They continued along the wash. This time they stepped a couple inches wider than before. They reached one hundred and found the second dead tree, this time on the left. The gnarled twins weren't alone. Around the bend lay a valley of dead trees. Askew limbs lay like discarded bones waiting for a prophet to speak life into them.

Rise, he wanted to say with the power of an ancient warrior.

Instead he let out a deep breath. It didn't come from the last time he inhaled, but it was air he'd held onto since getting Coyote Joe's note. He'd never admit his original doubts to Devin. The white boy didn't need to know his fear. The old warrior kept his promise. Everything he said would be there existed, down to the flat rock surrounded by twelve smaller ones. Jimmy's new life was about to begin.

CHAPTER 28

Q: Do people still dig for dinosaurs?
A: Yes. In fact, opportunities exist for regular people
to participate in excavating bones for museums.

The rain started as soon as Jimmy tipped over the stone. Joy stretched across his face with force. He moved the other twelve rocks from his path. He chose weaving bands over planting seeds, but the smell of dirt mixed with the wet night air stirred his growing excitement.

"It's raining." Devin whined.

"But we're here." He pulled out the small, fold-up shovel. The blade cut the earth and loosen the hard soil. The tool tinged against rocks that needed to be wedged free. He was inches away. And not the metaphorical kind of inches. Beneath this dirt, success called to him. Coyote Joe's promise waited patiently for Jimmy to dig it up.

The rain started in small drops.

"We've got to go." Devin sounded like he was about to die.

Coward. "Come on." He turned to him. "This isn't enough water to flood a toilet."

"You can't see upstream."

"If you're worried then quit moving your light from the hole."

They weren't going anywhere yet. Jimmy embraced the rain. A sign from heaven. An anointing, baptizing, blessing from God to him. The wet dirt on his hands and knees had been walked on by his ancestors. This land, his land, remained preserved by a white government. Federally protected pictographs dotted a former Ute playground. In this place, he wasn't a minority. He wouldn't be incorrectly judged.

"What was that?" Devin whispered from the other side of the hole.

Jimmy heard the twig snap. But he couldn't be worried about skunks right now. He plunged his shovel down into the hole again. A ding echoed from the earth, metal against metal, not metal against stone.

"I hit something."

"A rock."

"This sounded different."

Devin pulled away from the hole. "Something's out there." The dead trees and living shrubs around them appeared in the short beam weakened by the rain. "It's moving slow and toward us."

Jimmy didn't see anything. He placed his shovel on the ground and reached into the hole.

Stones.

Thick clay.

Random twigs.

Rain plopped heavy onto his bare back.

"Let's get out of here," Devin pleaded.

Jimmy ignored him. He wouldn't leave the treasure behind for a mountain lion or a flood. He shoved his hands into the earth and clawed blindly. Clay coated his skin. He couldn't see anything, but he wrapped two fingers around what felt like thin steel.

"It's a handle."

He yanked up.

The container attached to the handle wobbled but didn't budge.

"It's still stuck."

A flash of lightning brightened the landscape, followed two

seconds later by a loud boom. The storm had moved closer to them. They weren't quite out of the wash, but he kept digging. Besides, the thick drops on his skin didn't guarantee they'd be enough to create a river.

He fumbled his fingers over the smooth surface of what felt like a box. One side wiggled free while the ground continued to grip the other. The small plops of rain splashed more frequently on his bare back.

"We should get to higher ground." Devin stood as if to leave.

"I've almost got it." Jimmy knelt by the hole and loosened the dirt on the wedged side of the box. Coyote Joe's trophy. The prize. A ticket to the reservation rested within his reach and he couldn't leave it here. "Come on, flash the light down there. Just a couple more shovels and we won't have to come back."

Devin's beam returned to the open hole.

Jimmy worked with both the shovel and his hand to free the buried treasure.

The hole went dark again.

Oh brother. Yanking on Devin's sleeve he said, "Devin, come on! We're almost done."

Devin moved. "I tell you something's out there." His flashlight spanned across the blacken canyon.

"Whatever." He'd finish without him. He found his treasure. At this point, only a very strong beast could yank him away from this hole. As drops continue to wet his skin, he wrestled with the earth until it released the buried treasure.

"Not whatever. You have no idea what could be following us—"

"I've got it." Jimmy cut Devin off. "I've got it." He lifted a rusted brown cashbox above his head. The clouds opened up and the rain showered down. "Devin?" Jimmy hugged the cashbox to his chest. His friend hadn't made a sound.

Jimmy stood in the dark night.

"Devin?"

The white boy was gone, and with him Jimmy's confidence. This victorious moment turned eerie. He shouldered his backpack and picked up his flashlight. A bright blaze of lightning lit up the canyon. The white boy huddled behind a dead tree didn't grab his attention. Instead, as the thunder cracked through the sky, the six-foot-three-inch silhouette of Deputy Benson stood twenty yards up the wash.

CHAPTER 29

Q: *How fast can a dinosaur run?*
A: *That would vary based on the size and structure of each
animal. Undoubtedly some would have been very fast.*

Bushes snapped.

Branches broke.

Warnings shouted into the dark night with the thunder.

Devin warned Jimmy. He should have listened. But the dig
buried all thoughts of enemy number one into a place deep
below the treasure. Distraction had a way of disarming the best
of men. He'd been guilty twice now and both times related to
the same demon. How stupid was that? He pointed the
flashlight toward the deputy. Rain slashed across the beam. The
man with two different colored eyes appeared as ghostly as
ever.

"Run," Devin screamed. Lightning emphasized the heavy
downpour followed by a quick clap of thunder. The white man
lunged for Jimmy who darted away. Devin remained huddled
behind the dead tree. Smart strategy. Jimmy dropped the
cashbox next to his friend and took off. The deputy would
pursue Jimmy first. Let him.

A tree branch stretched across the path.

Jimmy slowed down to duck and the deputy caught hold of

his ankle.

Nasty demon. But the adventure couldn't end this way. Not with the goal so close. He kicked his other foot a couple of times before he made contact.

The devil yelled.

The grip on Jimmy's leg released.

He nailed him.

A bright flash of lightning revealed blood gushing from the white man's nose.

Boom! The thunder laughed.

Take that! Jimmy scrambled to his feet as rain multiplied. His flashlight beam bounced down the wash toward the mountain wall. "RUN!" He screamed back at Devin. The rumble of something bigger than the deputy roared from up the wash. Did the white man bring a posse? Jimmy couldn't worry about that right now. He needed to get out. Get free.

Slippery rocks and soggy sand slowed his pace. Wet jeans stuck to his legs. Heavy showers dripped into his eyes and down his loose braid. Everything on earth fought him and he had to win. Had to. He shook the excess drops from his head. Darkness and the deputy and a flood of water pursued him.

His cheeks and chest froze from the torrent. His flashlight didn't reach far into the wash. Drops blinked across the feeble light. Devin had been right. This place in the rain was more dangerous that he could have ever imagined. He trudged a few steps forward, a bright flash of lightning provided a better view. Ahead of him, the trail climbed a small hill. He must have passed trail marker number ten. He was on his way home. He didn't know how fast the deputy would regain his senses. Sooner, no doubt, than later.

Behind him the earth's stomach growled. The snapping and crackling of branches accompanied an awful roar. He climbed the small hill and clung to extended branches only to have his fingers slip away as a fast stream of knee-deep water yanked him off the clay mountain edge.

"God! Help!" he called before falling face first. He swallowed a mouthful of dirty water for his effort.

He was down.

The shallow current flowed too fast to allow him a strong foothold.

It tripped and pushed him.

With all his might, he tried to stand. The strength of the flood matched that of football linebackers. His feet sunk deep into the dark clay or slipped on smooth rocks. It couldn't end like this. It couldn't. A tree limb tore a scratch across his shoulder as he tried to twist himself forward. Rocks on the bottom banged bruises into his knees and arms. He reached for a tree. In a searing burst of pain, the rough bark tore the flesh from his hand.

He gripped his wrist and howled at the night sky. Rain pelted his face and tongue and sunk into his very soul. Ahead of him a log laid across the wash. The rushing water flowed under the space between the tree and ground. If he flipped his body around before he slammed into the thick wood, he might just escape this raging river.

"Someone! Help! God! HELP ME!"

The tree grew closer.

He twisted.

The water fought him.

This had to work. With his feet plunged into the sandy bed, he slammed into the trunk and leaned hard against the fallen tree. Yes. The current raised his body first, then tried to fold him over and suck him under the log. No. He held his breath then turned to the side. He hugged the tree with both arms, keeping his flashlight gripped in his right hand. Can't lose that. Can't lose the one source of light he had left. He tightened his fingers on the plastic handle. He tightened his arms around the fallen trunk. He tightened his heart into never letting go.

A small shrub assaulted him before it got sucked under the tree. The extended branches slowed the current enough for him to swing his right leg over the top of the tree. A break at last.

He pulled the left side of his body from the water. He straddled the large trunk bareback and hugged it like he would have hugged his mother at this moment. The suction tore his backpack from his shoulder, but he didn't care. The tree and his survival were more important than anything he had in the bag.

He rested his head on the smooth wood as the bag churned through the water like clothes in a washer. He had no desire to follow it. The flashlight continued to shine. The rubber cover protected the batteries, and his hope.

A weak cry came to him from up stream. Jimmy turned his head and pointed the beam toward the current. It couldn't be Devin. The boy would have to be ahead of him, wouldn't he?

Raging rapids churned with debris.

Another groan burst through the noisy storm.

A body crashed into his leg and yanked at him like a demon from hell.

CHAPTER 30

Q: *Could dinosaurs swim?*
A: *Evidence doesn't support swimming*
as natural to a dinosaur's existence.

Jimmy fought back the urge to pound the person and aimed his beam right into the face of Devin. Thank God. The best person he could have hoped for. He stuffed the flashlight into his waistband. With one hand wrapped around the tree, Jimmy grabbed Devin's jacket with the other.

The suction pulled Devin's shoulder underneath the log. The boy's face became submerged. Oh God. He couldn't watch his new friend drown right here in front of him. Devin's legs flailed from underneath the tree. Jimmy gathered his strength. More than life, he needed to save Devin from the hungry stream.

"Please, God, help me . . . pull . . . him . . . up.

He grunted out the last two words.

"I . . . don't . . . want . . . him . . . to . . . die!"

With a forceful tug, he pulled Devin up high enough for his friend to breathe. The torrent yanked on the kid and Jimmy's grip on the jacket loosened. In the next instant, Devin became sucked back under the water. No. His body sucked under the tree. Twisting in the newly formed stream, Devin's legs gave out in the now thigh-high river.

The kid stood for a blink only to be pushed over again by the stream that churned the backpack only moments ago. This was worse. This was much worse. Jimmy pulled his flashlight from where he tucked it and scanned the area. The torrential darkness prevented his beam from reaching even a few feet forward.

"Devin!" Pouring rain swallowed the sound.

Eyes closed, he tipped his head back and screamed, "DEVIN!"

Nothing but the flood's roar responded.

His legs gripped the tree as a branch slammed into his thigh. The raging water threatened to pull him down. He fought and kicked the monster with every muscle.

He shivered and then cursed himself for doing it.

"Please, God! No matter . . . what—

. . . keep . . . Devin . . . alive."

He didn't know what lay beyond the natural eye. Supernatural experiences had presented themselves to him before. To deny the existence of spiritual forces bigger than humans was narrow-minded and stubborn. But up until this moment, he never felt the desire to know God's name. His real name.

As the raging flood pulled at him, he wanted to know his deity personally.

Even if he or she or it was white.

He laid flat and hugged the tree. With his face pointed away from the flood, he closed his eyes. He only ever prayed when danger overwhelmed him. He only ever sought a God when he needed a superhero. He continued to utter pleas of safety for Devin more than for himself.

"He never wanted to come. And I forced him." He spoke to the wet bark. He mumbled and begged as he inched his way toward the bank. Rain mixed with the tears on his cheek. If Devin got hurt it would be his fault. "God, if you are listening. I will give up the box, the trip to the reservation, my own life for Devin's. Please."

He didn't expect life to play fair. His prayers to kill had been answered—he had to hope his prayers could save in this moment. He did more than ask, he believed. He had to. He needed to break his silence to God, the way he'd broken his silence to white men. So, he asked and asked again until he thought he'd imagined the rain ease up. Either that, or the icy pings on his back hit numb skin. The rushing current continued to gnaw against his legs, but the sky had let up. Time to get Devin.

He scooted forward.

The boy had to be alive.

He scooted again.

The boy had to be alive.

He scooted once more and his head bumped against the muddy bank.

He pushed himself up. Devin would live. The tree surface slipped beneath him, so he knelt and balanced his weight, grabbing a jutting juniper bush. A strong yank indicated the shrub would hold him. With his foot on the dirt wall, he leaned back and repelled.

Beneath him something crashed into the log he just abandoned. He didn't look back. He couldn't. Something about the thud reminded him of Devin's arrival. Jimmy couldn't look for fear it would be the deputy. The idea sent a tremor through him.

This whole adventure had been reckless. In the back of his mind, where history lay next to reality, he began to wonder if it was worth it. Life for him would never be easy. Coyote Joe's quest couldn't change that. Yet here he was risking his life and Devin's—for what? He shook his head and grasped another bush. With his foot on the juniper, he could lay his stomach on the wet trail. He'd get Devin and figure out life later.

A two-handed push-up got his body high enough to place his knee on the bank. He scrambled to his feet. The kid might have climbed up by now, or still be in the stream below. With his left hand he kept balance, while the flashlight surveyed the rushing water for any sign of his friend.

"Devin!" Rain muffled his voice, but he continued to search.

No doubt the cashbox had been lost, which made the entire adventure even more meaningless. A man's journey. What a joke. He had behaved like a reckless child. The deputy could be scaling the mud wall behind him. Unless—

An involuntary idea overcame him.

What if the deputy had drowned?

He stopped and pointed his flashlight behind him. No sign of the stalker. Had he added another white man to his list? Dad. Boyfriend number one. Drunk Dean, and now Deputy Benson. This would never end. Even when he wasn't wishing white men dead, he still might have killed one. He couldn't think about that right now. He had to find Devin. He'd already killed too many people—he couldn't live with himself if Devin died.

He pushed away the thoughts.

"NO!" He shouted to the sky.

"NO!" He shouted to the canyon.

"NO!" He shouted to God. "Devin will live."

CHAPTER 31

Q: *Were all dinosaurs giants?*
A: *No, most dinosaurs aren't*
bigger than animals known today.

Jimmy scrambled through the bushes doing his best to keep his footing. His flashlight panned as the rain became thinner. After what felt like an eternity, he found Devin plastered to a tree.

"Climb," Jimmy yelled.

Devin's arms didn't look scrawny now. The tattooed snake flexed as the scrappy kid remained glued to the tree trunk. His legs trembled and while Jimmy could see a strength in Devin he hadn't recognized before, not even the strongest man in the world would last long down there for much longer.

"I'm coming," Jimmy shouted

In the narrow light of his flashlight beam, Jimmy studied the tall cottonwood. Its dark limbs dripped with the constant rain. Jumping onto the tree could put them both into more danger. More trouble. He couldn't risk Devin's one opportunity for rescue. His friend was alive right now. No one, not Pyen or Devin's Gram, knew where they were. With the deputy probably lying face down in the stream, water seeping into his broken nose, the devil wouldn't be able to injure anyone again or go for help.

The flood would keep both hikers and rangers away from this trail for days. Someone might find their bikes, but a search party would come too late. Based on the trembling boy at the bottom of the tree, Jimmy didn't have a choice.

Devin couldn't survive the night in the rushing stream.

Tomorrow would just have to worry about tomorrow.

He wiggled one of the branch limbs.

Sturdy.

He put his weight on it.

Slippery.

He straddled the branch and shimmied his way to the trunk. Maybe all that worry should have been used before they ever entered this crazy adventure. Now, Devin needed to be saved, just like Pyen and Coyote Joe. As much as he wanted to feel sorry for his pathetic life, he couldn't until he got Devin safe. He slid-climbed to the branch closest to the boy.

He decided to try an old elementary-school-jungle-gym trick. From back during his life with the beast. He wasn't fat yet when he used to sit on a branch and let his butt sink until he could hang from the crooks of his knees and his hands. Before he knew it, his feet wrapped around the branch and he let go of his hands and hung upside-down.

The trick worked then.

The trick worked now.

Rain dripped down into his face. He couldn't see, but he felt Devin's head and eventually his arm.

"Grab my arms and climb."

"It's too slippery."

"Use me as leverage."

Devin tried. After six staggered attempts, Jimmy decided to change plans.

"Wait." He grabbed Devin's left hand and wrapped it around his chest. "Hold on to me like I'm going to give you a piggy-back ride."

Devin's right arm twisted across Jimmy's neck, cutting off his air. He scrambled and clawed until Devin released his grasp.

"I can't do it." His friend clung to the tree trunk. Jimmy tried to ignore the water on the boy's face. He told himself Devin wasn't frightened to tears. It was rain. His friend would be fine.

"Listen!" The blood raced to Jimmy's head and increased its thumping. "I'm here. I won't let you die." This had to end well. It had to. A dead deputy would be burden enough for one night. He would die himself before he let Devin. "Grab my pits, not my neck."

Devin let go of the tree and wrapped himself around Jimmy with his hands locked together around Jimmy's chest.

Jimmy grabbed the branch and hoisted his friend up high enough to reach the limb. He curled his fingers in to one of Devin's belt loops and pulled the boy's leg toward the tree.

"Whoa!"

"Kick your leg over the branch." Jimmy lifted his chin to release the head rush.

Devin kicked his leg. The boy's foot landed against the back of Jimmy's head.

"Wait." Jimmy yelled. He pulled himself up to straddle the branch. "Okay, try again."

This time Devin's foot reached the tree limb. Finally, Jimmy didn't know how much longer he could hold on. His head hurt.

"Kick your leg over."

Devin locked his leg around the branch.

"Good! Now climb up."

The kid shoved his foot forward only to hit Jimmy square in the crotch.

CHAPTER 32

Q: Did dinosaurs cry?
A: Animals don't feel the same emotions as
humans, but most have tear ducts to wet their eyes.

Scratches.

Scrapes.

Bruises in private places. All of them made themselves completely known once Devin and Jimmy found a small ledge to huddle under. Jimmy's wet jeans clung to him like the extra hundred pounds he used to carry. Devin shivered as Jimmy faced the reality of what just happened. He'd saved a life.

The kid looked like he'd been hit by a train, but two thoughts pushed their way to the front of his consciousness. One, he'd saved Devin's life. The amazing feeling replaced any other he could ever think of. The second thought troubled him more.

Deputy Benson.

For the first time he wasn't wondering where the man was, but how he was.

Jimmy didn't want to carry the burden of another dead man. He never wanted to destroy others, he just didn't want to be destroyed by them. Based on the loud crack and gushing blood, he'd definitely broken the man's nose. Probably not enough to kill him, but enough to disable him in the flood.

He stared up the dark canyon and tried to remember if he'd said anything during the last twenty-four hours about wanting the man dead. No matter how many soggy trees or muddy paths he focused on, he couldn't remember verbalizing a death wish. If the man died, this might be the first skeleton he'd hang in his closet that wasn't made from a prayer or wish.

The idea that his enemy could be face down under the flood troubled him. He pictured random branches crashing against the deputy's head, all because of him. But what could he do? The idea of going back and saving the man wouldn't let him go. The thought clung to him like his rain-soaked pants.

Since he never begged God to bring his own father home alive, why would he save the deputy? If he didn't push open his bedroom door in the burning apartment in Puyallup, why would he risk a trip upstream for a whack-job who'd stalked and threatened him? This entire night would have been so much easier if the deputy had left Jimmy alone. He picked up a rock and chucked it into the spontaneous stream.

Maybe it was the actual physical contact he'd had with the white man that troubled him. All the other deaths didn't require a punch or a kick. Guilt reminded him that if the man was safe, he would have slammed into the same tree they had. The deputy would have caught up to them during the struggle to save Devin. Tonight was his chance at changing his life. His destiny. He couldn't start it with another name on his list. All this time he'd thought it was about Coyote Joe and a now-lost treasure. But his heart thumped hard with the knowledge that the only person who could save Jimmy from this curse of death was Jimmy.

"I have to go back."

"Where?" Devin's voice quivered.

"To the dig."

"No, you don't."

He knew Devin wouldn't understand, he didn't understand it fully himself. The man was a menace. Everything inside said stay, except the nagging reality of future guilt. "I don't want this entire trip to be a waste of time."

Devin didn't say anything. Instead, he slowly lifted up his

shirt and began to untie a wet string.

"What are you doing?"

He knelt by his friend to get a better look. In the glare of battery-operated light, Devin's bootlaces were looped through the handle on the top of the box, then wrapped around Devin's narrow waist and tied it in about a hundred knots.

"What did you do?" Jimmy examined the raw flesh on Devin's sides where the wet laces rubbed his skin away. This couldn't be happening.

"It was important to you. So, while you fought the deputy, I grabbed it."

Devin saved Coyote Joe's cashbox. In the middle of a flash flood. The boy risked his life to make sure that Jimmy got what he came for.

Crap.

Crap.

Crap. Why couldn't life be easy? Devin's sacrifice was unbelievable. Instead of relief, a rush of guilt poured over Jimmy. He hated himself for making a thing more important than a person.

"Why would you do that?" He bit his lip. "I wasn't going back for that stupid box. Come on, I'm not that lame." A pain, deeper than his skin, cut through him. Maybe he was that lame. Devin never wanted to come on this adventure. He hated the dark and dead things and all of this. Devin accepted this journey for one reason and one reason only.

He was a friend.

A real friend.

This white boy wasn't a temporary high school experience, but someone he would trust for the rest of his life. If Devin became a mean, angry white man, Jimmy would be there to fight him down. To remind him of this moment. For the rest of forever, the two of them would become different than their history predicted.

"Sit back." Jimmy gently untied the burden that should have been his. His fingers felt fat and uncoordinated against the tight knots. The moist strings wouldn't budge and the skin at Devin's side began to bleed. The kid would leave this adventure with sacrificial scars, something to be proud of, all Jimmy had was leftover skunk and scratches.

"Let me get my pocket knife."

He swallowed a lump as his fingers wiggled into his wet pocket.

He sawed the string with a gentle urgency. On the seventh slice, the lace snapped. Devin exhaled a deep sigh. Jimmy fought the urge to hurl the box into the churning water below. He would have done it, but that would have made Devin's injuries pointless. A shiver shook him from his core. The best thing to do was tie the laces into a pack he'd carry on his own.

"So, what did you want to go back for?" Devin asked.

Jimmy sank against the mountain. His motives had become blurred like pictographs on a clay wall. "To check on the deputy."

Devin didn't say anything.

"I wanted to make sure he's alive."

The rain continued its sad dripping. Jimmy fingered the lock on the brown cashbox. A cursed treasure, like everything else in his life.

"Did you hit your head on a rock?" Devin finally said.

"No."

"A branch then."

"No," he huffed.

"You definitely cracked your thick skull."

"I didn't."

"Then why in the world did we risk our lives to enter this God-forsaken canyon? You wanted to save your mother from that whack job."

He agreed with everything Devin said, so he stated his lingering problem. "I don't want to be the reason he died."

"You aren't."

"I broke his nose."

"Defending yourself." Devin shook his head. "He followed us." The kid winced at the pain in waist. After a moment he said emphatically. "The man snuck up on us without a warning. If he's hurt, it's his own fault. No different than if I would have been washed away with that stream. I chose to come here. You didn't make me. And you didn't make him."

The words contained logic, but guilt continued to make him hesitate. "He could be dying."

"And so could we." Devin leaned toward him. He winced from the pain in his side. "Do you know that both of my parents drown? Did you?"

"No." Jimmy pulled back. The memory of meeting the boy in the cemetery suddenly made sense. His parents. Dead. Drowned. He exhaled.

"Yeah. Water is dangerous. It's a killer. Besides, that deputy could be anywhere by now. You saw how far that current dragged us. Even if you did go back, where would you look? Give me a break. I'm not fighting that flood again. Not tonight. Not ever."

Jimmy rubbed his forehead to push away the frustration. He wanted clarity. He wanted in this moment to know, with certainty what he should do. A rumble happened far to the East. Obviously, the dark night agreed with Devin.

"We're not going back." Devin leaned against the rock wall. "We have our own skins to save. And whether you believe it or not, we're worth it."

CHAPTER 33

Q: Are dinosaur tracks hard to find?
A: The footprints of dinosaurs are more
common than full fossil skeletons.

Jimmy stayed with Devin. What else could he do? The kid almost died last night. It was more important to support Devin than his own desires at the moment. The rain had stopped. The cashbox bounced against his back as they navigated the slowly subsiding flood.

The wet shoelaces rubbed blisters into his shoulders where the skin had softened. The stupid package weighed more than the entire night. Less than a sunset ago, an adventure meant more to him than human life. In fact, as much as he hated white men, this trip taught him how close he was to becoming exactly like the thing he despised.

Hadn't his own father wanted his needs met more than caring for the feelings of others? Jimmy wasn't any different. The idea that Jimmy had sacrificed so much in a single night made the Coyote-Joe treasure tainted. A large part of his heart just wanted to dump it. Pretend that he'd never been as greedy for control as his father had been. Pretend he didn't use Pyen as an excuse. Just like Dad.

The wash opened up at the base of the trail, their sneakers

squeaked as they stepped over wet rocks. The water spread out in different directions. Most of the flow surged toward the river. Their bikes were pushed past the place where they'd left them, too big to be lifted up onto the road or through the pipe below the road. Devin found them and in good condition. They'd been dragged a hundred yards beyond where they'd left them. A hundred yards closer to Devin's Gram's house, thank goodness.

He half thought of leaving the box to drown in the same stream as the deputy, but he couldn't. Devin deserved more than that. No, Jimmy would just have to carry his reward as a symbol of his quest for control. In fact, that was probably a great idea. Whatever was in the box would be a constant reminder to leave the power business to someone else. He'd still go to the reservation, but not on the stacked bodies of any more people.

His tired legs pedaled him forward, under the pre-sunrise sky. The spray from Devin's wheels kicked up puddles until they got back to the shed near the house. They couldn't keep the bikes out without raising questions. Better to put them back where Devin's grandparents thought they'd been all night.

Even after the heavy rain, the inside of the tent was surprisingly dry. The snoring cellphone had a dead battery. But it didn't matter, the deputy was gone. Jimmy peeled off his wet clothes and slipped into the dry sleeping bag. Comfortable and warm, he decided to ask Devin one last question "Why did you say that?"

"Say what?" Devin rolled his face toward the tent wall.

"Back there on the trail."

"Could you be a little more specific?"

"You talked about how I should live whether I thought I was worth it or not?" Jimmy didn't like how close Devin had been to being right. The kid slunk into the hidden parts of him and tried to bring non-existent weaknesses to the surface. "I'm not suicidal."

"It didn't mean anything."

"Then why say it?"

"Can't we just get some sleep, please?"

"I need to know." And he did. He needed to know if his insecurity leaked out and stained the way the world saw him.

"Do you think I don't value myself?"

"Of course you do." Devin curled up tighter into his bag. "I said it because I didn't want to go back and rescue that dumb deputy. Now let it go."

Jimmy didn't answer.

He didn't add follow-up questions.

But he didn't let it go either. Not inside. Not where he thought he had everything locked up tight. An invasion of his thoughts would reveal his true fears. Devin knew too much about him already.

But the white boy had abandoned the deputy to die, same as Jimmy. They now shared a skeleton. What would that be like? He wanted to study that more, but fatigue rolled over him. He counted the rain drops until the chirp of birds woke him.

Hours erased by sleep had passed.

The fresh smell of grass revealed the night had provided the kind of rain that lured worms onto the pavement only to bake them in the morning sun. The new day glared through the tent walls, pretending that the horrible night had never happened. Life was like that. It went on every day as if there weren't a dead deputy in a washed-out canyon. He turned in his sleeping bag. Life went on as if there wasn't a kid somewhere in the world curled up in fear from the anger that lived with him. Life went on as if abuse was only on Dr. Phil.

The cashbox stared at him like a rectangular idol. Two small screws in the lock hinge stared like unblinking eyes. A brass, padlock nose bent over the long straight mouth where the box could be opened. He no longer wanted to make the box yawn wide and tell its secrets. He didn't care about a totem anymore. He no longer believed he'd ever really get free.

He dragged the box next to him and fingered the latch.

"Did Coyote Joe give you the key?" Devin mumbled from the other side of the tent.

"Nope."

"Then we should break it open."

"Whatever." Jimmy was tired of fighting. He didn't want to continue to tie himself to this adventure. The night had already bonded him to disaster in ways impossible to sever. Devin didn't know the burden that came with dead men. "I need to get home."

"Why?"

He set the box back down. The overwhelming urge to be seven years old and safe surfaced. Vulnerability crept over him. He pushed against it and sat up, keeping the thick down of his sleeping bag over his shoulders. He didn't care. He wanted to. He wanted to succeed. But the invasion of death had ruined his adventure. While he loved the already dead, he didn't like to watch things die. And chances were high that the deputy was dead. He couldn't pinpoint when the enemy stopped being evil and returned to human form. The dark night and wet sky had changed everything.

"I need to check on Pyen."

Devin sat up. His sleeping bag crumpled around him. "You're not still worried about the deputy, are you?"

Jimmy wrapped the quilted bag tighter around his naked shoulders.

"He's fine." Devin continued, "Nobody dies of a broken nose."

"Yes, they do. Happens in ultimate fighting all the time."

"We almost died in that flood last night." The kid looked angry. It was the first time Jimmy had really caught any fire in the boy's eyes. "You don't even watch ultimate fighting."

Devin was guessing and he was right. But so what. Jimmy didn't need to watch to know that the deputy was seriously injured. If he wasn't, he would have followed them. Found them. Captured them.

"Look, we're alive," Devin continued. "And that no-good deputy got to higher ground too. What we need to do is find out what's in that box." He kicked his way out of his bag. "I'll be right back."

Jimmy reached for his jeans. Cold and damp denim sent chills through him. He should have brought an extra pair. He scooted his bag over to Devin's side of the tent. He'd rummaged a warm sweatshirt from his friend's stash. One size too small, the hoodie barely came to his waist, but the warmth made the awkward worth it. Devin returned with a bolt cutter.

"Are you serious?" The monstrous thing came to Devin's hip.

His friend just grinned and leaned on it like a cane.

"Why in the world would your grandpa even own one of those?"

"To cut chain link."

The tiny lock didn't have a chance against the beast. The metal snapped off before Jimmy could give it another thought.

Devin placed the tool on the tent floor.

Jimmy pulled at the sweatshirt.

They exchanged glances then looked back at the box.

"What do you think's in there?" Anticipation seeped through Devin's voice.

"I told you, I don't care."

"Well, I do." Devin bit his bottom lip. Then he peeked over at Jimmy like a kid at Christmas. "Open it."

Jimmy sat back on his rumpled sleeping bag and shrugged. He leaned over and without bravado, opened the lid. He didn't look in the box. In fact, he turned away not wanting to see what lay inside. Too many disasters had happened on this journey, he didn't want this to be another one.

"No way." Devin's voice dropped.

"What?"

"Look and see."

"You don't sound too excited."

"I'm not."

Jimmy turned toward the box. It had two sections. The left side had a closed lid while in the open half on the right rattled some brown seeds and a distorted green plant. Shaped like a green, farm-grown tomato with cactus-like skin. "What is it?"

"Peyote."

"Peyote? Like peace pipe weed?"

"Yeah."

Without an invitation, his PlayStation came to mind. The words of a possibly dead deputy echoed from an unwanted place and flowed out of Jimmy's mouth, "The man is a drug addict."

"You think?" Devin shouted.

He shook his head. "Never mind." He slammed the lid to the box down and wrapped his arms in a knot against his chest.

Soft words came from outside the tent. "What stinks?"

Jimmy stuffed the cash box under his pillow while Devin stashed the broken lock and bolt cutter under his bag.

"Who crapped their pants?" Devin's ten-year-old brother unzipped the flap.

Jimmy pulled himself up. He'd forgotten all about the skunk smell. His nose didn't even register the stink any more.

Devin didn't move.

"Gram said to come in for lunch. But you stink."

"Fine. You told us, now go away."

"No!"

"Go away before I punch you!" Jimmy raised his fist.

"I'm telling." The ten-year-old waved his hand in front of his nose and ran toward the house.

"You weren't really going to hit him, were you?"

"No," Jimmy laughed. "The boy ran to tattle last time, I guessed he'd do it again."

"Good guess."

The tent door flapped open. Birds chirped. The late morning air brought the smell of baked bread. The homemade scent resurrected a simpler time. A Pyen-and-Jimmy-unhurried time between white men in his mother's life. A place where the universe invited them to sit still after a nightshift at the bakery. Those small windows of life with just his mother and him. Those small, always broken, windows.

"That was close," Devin whispered.

Jimmy didn't answer.

Devin crawled toward the opening and the lunch his Gram prepared. "You need to get rid of that thing."

Jimmy couldn't agree more, but how? Oh God. How could every single thing in his life turn out for crap? Not only had he killed the deputy last night, he did it by trusting a no-account Indian. He shook his head. Wasn't the world hard enough?

CHAPTER 34

Q: Were paleontologists ever mistaken about dinosaurs?
A: The Brontosaurus never existed. It was molded from the
skull of an Apatosaurus and the body of a Diplodocus.

Devin's grandparents had a ton of questions. Devin hesitated, not wanting to lie and it was Jimmy's turn to save his friend.

"We decided to go out into the rain last night only to get caught by a skunk and fall into a fire-ant pit."

"Wow!" Devin's Gram looked impressed.

The old man's cell phone rang. He held a short conversation while studying the two boys. Maybe the deputy's body had already been found. "Yeah," he drawled into his phone. "Both boys are here, eating lunch."

Jimmy stared at the thick sandwich, anxiety pushed hunger away from his stomach. Was he about to be caught? Hauled off to juvie?

"Sure, we'll call you when he starts to head home." The man clicked off his phone and approached the table.

"Was that Jimmy's mother?" Devin's Gram asked.

"Yeah." The old man stared hard at them. "Why'd you guys go into the rain last night?" It was a solid accusation.

The old woman flicked a hand at her husband. "They're

boys, aren't they?" The questions ended. The old man left them to scarfed-down lunch. Jimmy's mother called. Why would she call? Once the dishwasher was loaded, Devin's Gram put baking-soda paste on their ant bites and washed Jimmy's hair with tomato juice in the kitchen sink.

By the expression on Devin's little brother's face, it didn't help much.

No big deal. Jimmy was ready to go home.

Back in the tent, he rolled the cashbox into his sleeping bag. He'd find a way to deal with Coyote Joe. Maybe not today, but soon. Devin offered to bike half of the ten miles home.

"We'll take the back part of Brush Creek Road."

Jimmy shrugged. The blisters on his shoulders burned. The wounds on his arms and legs cut deeper than his skin. The fire-ant bites itched like mosquito bites to the tenth power. The first five hundred yards pulled aches from his calves and thighs. The night's battle was over. He was ready to escape the weary landscape and sleep in his own bed.

Not that the trailer promised relief, but he was even too tired to worry about that. According to Devin, if the deputy had died, his body would have fallen well past the marked Sound of Silence trail. He lay too far off track for anyone to find him except for the animals. Pyen would think he'd abandoned her. Until the sheriff's department came by asking questions.

"We should tell someone."

"Yeah." Devin wove his bike back and forth next to Jimmy. The road had dried in the afternoon sun. Small puddles in the shade of weary cottonwoods remained as the only evidence of last night's deluge. "I'll make an anonymous call."

"How? They trace those you know."

"Oh, yeah. They do." They fell into silence again.

"What about a note?"

"Good idea."

"But, what if he's alive?"

Devin's question sent prickles up Jimmy's arm. He half hoped and half dreaded the idea. The deputy would put Jimmy in jail for assault. And Pyen would be alone.

They stopped at the bottom of the big hill, right before Brush

Creek forked.

"I can go the rest of the way alone," Jimmy said, and stuck out his hand. It seemed odd and grown-up, but right somehow. They'd matured in the last twelve hours in ways Jimmy could never pull back from.

"See you around."

"For sure." Jimmy let go of Devin's hand and started to pedal hard toward Vernal. He hoped to get home before any news of last night got there first. Pyen would have said something if the news had reached her. She would have insisted on talking to Jimmy. But she didn't. He was safe for now. Dead or alive, news of the deputy would reach him sooner or later.

At the trailer park, the old lady in number two pinched her nose as he rolled past her. "What happened to you?"

He didn't answer. He'd heard about his awful scent from enough people already.

He locked his bike at the back of the trailer. Pyen must have heard him because she stood in the doorway as he approached.

"Whoa." She stepped back.

"I know, I know." Jimmy said it first. "I smell like skunk."

She stepped out of his way as he climbed inside.

"You need a hydrogen peroxide solution."

"Devin's Gram used tomato juice."

"That doesn't work." She pushed him deeper into the house.

"Great." He didn't care anymore. He just wanted to creep into bed and wait for the world to come crashing down on him.

"And where is your backpack?"

"I tossed it."

"We could have washed it."

He shrugged. Left-over skunk drew so much attention.

"Those things cost money."

"I know, Pyen. I know." He followed his mother into the hall. She opened the linen closet and retrieved a brown bottle from her first-aid supplies.

"Hold these."

Jimmy took a gray plastic bucket and the hydrogen peroxide. Pyen went to the kitchen and came back with an orange box of baking soda and dish soap. "Get undressed and sit in the tub, but don't turn on the water."

He stepped over the tub and sat in his underwear while Pyen turned into a mad scientist. The concoction in the bucket fizzled and she handed it to him.

"Oh, Paa," Pyen leaned back. "Did you wrestle a bear or something?"

He pushed her hand away. "Devin and I messed around a bit."

"A skunk and this?"

He didn't answer. His mother shook her head. He could tell she wanted to ask a ton of questions, but she didn't. She bit her lip before finally saying, "Wash yourself with that mixture. Especially where the skunk hit you most."

Pyen gave him one last curious look, then pulled the shower curtain closed and left the room.

He shut his eyes and scrubbed his forehead first. The solution bubbled over his skin and stung open sores. He dipped his washrag into the solution and scrubbed the back of his neck. When the bucket was empty, he continued to sit in the tub while turning on the shower. His long hair dripped. The smell of skunk lifted. Warm water rained on him. Before he could draw peace from the moment, the bathroom door banged open.

"Get out here, NOW!" Through the shower curtain, Pyen's shadow had hands planted on wide hips.

"What'd I do?" He turned the faucet off. Well-rehearsed fear crept over him.

"Don't give me that NONSENSE!" She pulled the curtain back. With force, she extended one finger toward the door. "OUT! NOW!" She turned and slammed the door behind her.

What in the world?

Pyen didn't get angry. Whatever she heard must be bad. Which means she found out about the deputy. The white man might be in the living room right now. Unless he left word about his whereabouts and someone went out and found him. He could have had a radio.

He stood-up and grabbed a towel from the rack. He dropped his wet underwear into the bathtub. His bedroom was on the other side of the kitchen. A cat wouldn't fit through the bathroom window. Besides, Jimmy couldn't escape to the reservation naked.

He crept from the room with one towel wrapped around his waist and another over his shoulders. He feared facing the deputy now more than ever. The vulnerability of being unclothed. No fabric to separate the beating from bare flesh.

The floor creaked beneath his feet.

He reached the arch to the kitchen.

Pyen sat with her back to him.

Alone.

No deputy.

He rubbed his head, not only to dry his hair, but to settle his nerves. No deputy. Was that good or bad, he no longer knew. Oh, crap. He no longer knew anything. He didn't want the deputy dead, but he didn't want the man here either. Life wasn't supposed to be this complicated. His mother shouldn't be sitting at the table slumped over, her shoulders shaking. Her head hung toward the table. He hadn't seen his mother cry in a long time.

"Oh Lord," she sobbed. "What has he done?"

He froze. She knew. She knew about the killing. She knew all about his part in it. She loved the man, and now she knew he was guilty. Guilty of this death and hundreds of others. Maybe she found his list. She now knew just how dark his heart really was. His life was over in ways it never had been before.

He continued toward her.

She heard him because, in a flash, her posture straightened. With her back still to him, she wiped the tears from her face. After a firm tug on her shirt, she pulled her hand through her hair.

When she stood to face him, Jimmy saw what she'd found. It was worse. Impossible, but worse. This wasn't about the deputy. This wasn't about death. This wasn't about white men. In fact, Jimmy wondered if it might not have been better to have her find the list. Her tears weren't about any of that. This was about trust. On the table next to the paper napkin holder, Coyote Joe's box of drugs laid open.

CHAPTER 35

Q: *How were dinosaurs discovered?*
A: *An English museum owner, Robert Plot, described an enormous thigh bone he believed belonged to a giant, in 1676.*

"What have you done?"

Jimmy felt her defeat. The surrender in her voice. The flat tone of tiredness echoed in his bones. She didn't know about the deputy, instead, she thought he had discovered Indian weed. He needed to make sure she didn't believe he could be into this stuff. "It's just a plant we dug up."

"Do you think I'm stupid?"

"No." He fumbled toward her. "We found it, I promise."

"Oh, really."

"Yes." He tightened the towel at his waist and sat across from her. "I know peyote is illegal. I was going to get rid of it." He tried to make eye contact without luck, so he reached for her hands. She turned and walked to the sink. He followed.

"I'm not talking about the peyote." She wrung her hands. "I'm talking about the meth."

"Meth??" Jimmy almost dropped his towel. No way. He had checked the box at Devin's, it was only that cactus-like thing and some seeds. Nothing else really. Except. He couldn't really remember. He hadn't looked really hard because it didn't matter back then. He didn't care. But now he had to care. "I didn't see any meth in the box."

"I'm not stupid." Pyen screeched. Her hands were in fists. "Don't think I'm stupid."

"I'm not." He shook his head. She was wrong, she had to be. Devin would have seen it. Come on, Jimmy would have seen it. He would have gotten rid of the box for sure. There was no way the box had any—

Needles.

Baggies.

White powder.

Clear crystals.

A thick roll of cash.

It all lay on the table next to the box. The side compartment Jimmy and Devin didn't explore, now lay open. Oh, crap. He paced the floor. No way! Come one. This couldn't be happening. Was the deputy right all along? Had the dead stalker told him the truth? Even the worst of men will tell the truth sometimes. Coyote Joe had tricked him. Used him. Crackhead-wasted-old-man-loser! That piece of scrap sent Jimmy into the wilderness in the middle of the night to dig up his stash. Coyote Joe spent so long in the white world, he'd become equally cunning and deceitful.

"Why?" Pyen straightened her back, the anger returned to her eyes. "I rolled open your sleeping bag to clean off the skunk smell. I didn't expect to find this."

He slipped into a chair again. He didn't have an answer, not one she would like. Even though the drugs weren't his. She'd be just as disappointed to know how he had gotten them.

"Drugs?" Tears laced her voice. "This is bad, Jimmy, really bad. I can't fix this. I can't clean up this kind of mess."

"Pyen." He reached for her hand. "It's not mine."

"Then why hide it in your bag." Accusation filled her voice.

"I don't know." And he didn't. He had no idea why he hadn't chucked the whole thing into the creek on his way home. But then again, he did know. He wanted to confront Coyote Joe. Shove the stinking drugs into the old man's face. None of that mattered now. There would be nothing to shove. Not peyote.

Not meth. Not guilt. He needed to restore what he'd broken.

"We found it," he said, with the most sincere face he could manage.

"You found a strange box," her flat tone proved she didn't believe him, "wrapped it in your sleeping bag, dragged it all the way home without knowing what you had?"

"Yes." He reached for her hand and this time she let him hold it. He bounced his legs under the table. He didn't care to keep Coyote Joe's secret any longer. But if he said anything, she'd find out about the note, then the adventure and finally the dead deputy.

"I need to call Andrew."

"No," Jimmy tightened the grip on her hand.

"Ouch." She yanked away from him. "Stop that. I know you don't like him. But he'll know what to do."

Panic rose in Jimmy like the mercury in a thermometer.

"He's not a bad man." Pyen stood and straightened her shirt. "If this isn't yours, you have nothing to worry about."

She couldn't be more wrong. He got up slowly. He imagined wrestling the phone away from her as she leaned against the counter pressing the buttons on her phone, but he couldn't fight her like that. He was done. It was over.

He went to his room while his mother called the deputy. Or more precisely, the dead man's phone. Behind his closed door, he paced. Chills flushed his arms. Old memories of fear surged through his nerves. He rubbed his arms hard trying to forget what might be coming.

What an idiot. He should never have trusted the old man. He shouldn't have ever trusted anyone. Angry tears pushed hard to escape his eyes. He plopped face down on the bed. He shook his head back and forth. Through gritted teeth he said, "I don't understand. Why did my life have to suck so bad? I didn't choose this mess."

He crumpled his bedspread into his face. But the questions wouldn't be suffocated.

"Why'd my dad have to be such a jerk? An idiotic-violent-war-loving jerk."

A primal scream wafted through the fabric and vibrated the

bed.

"WHY?"

"WHY?"

The stabbing sense of hopelessness churned inside. People don't miss real dinosaurs. They miss what they wanted them to be. Jimmy was no different. Thoughts of his father thumped through him. Forget about Deputy Benson. Forget about Coyote Joe. Forget about Pyen. Where was the man who contributed the DNA that made him? Where was that man?

He let the sobs out. He didn't resist. Strange as it might sound, he suddenly missed the beast. Not the abuse, never that. He missed the good times. He missed the random good days.

Trips to the zoo.

A ten-piece bucket of KFC.

Go-karts and bumper cars.

More than anything else, he ached for the opportunity to see his father change. There used to be a chance that one day it would have gotten better. He let go of the real question he'd been asking all his life. "Why couldn't he love me?"

There was no hope.

Death was permanent.

He dug his fingers into his scalp wanting to pull his hair out from the roots. He climbed beneath the covers. Wrapped like a turtle in a shell, he shrunk his tall frame into a knot. And fought against the pain. Battled the unexplainable.

Why couldn't he be full? At the deepest core of his being, Jimmy wanted to be cared for, protected, supported. He wanted to be loved. But no. No. Never. For the rest of his entire life, death and defeat would pursue and consume him. He didn't ask to be rejected. Or abandoned by the man who created him. Why couldn't his heart let go of it? Come on, give it up. His father never loved him. Get over it.

But as much as his brain pleaded with his heart, the desire wouldn't abate.

He pounded his head against the pillows until his strength gave out.

The smell of Old Spice entered first. He didn't hear the tap on the door. He froze. Through the woven blue threads of his blanket, the fuzzy frame of a six-foot tall man leaned in the doorway.

Jimmy braced his naked body for his beating.

The door clicked shut. Pyen stood on the other side like she'd been on so many other days of his life. The difference this time. He deserved it. He couldn't remember a time he'd earned it more. And right now, a stick or extension cord or a fist might make him feel better. Ease the unyielding emotional pain.

Without waiting a moment longer, he pulled the covers off his head.

CHAPTER 36

Q: *Do dinosaurs regret killing?*
A: *Regret and empathy are emotions*
specific to the human condition.

The deputy didn't hit him. A thick white nose bridge confirmed the damage from last night. He didn't say anything except, "Let's go."

Jimmy didn't want to. He wanted to be five years old. He wanted to cling to his mother's skirt and peek around her legs at the problem. Instead, he got dressed and walked past Pyen who handed the white man Coyote Joe's stash.

Coyote Joe.

Unbelievable.

Life was hard enough for an Indian in a white man's world, he didn't need a worthless Indian to betray him. Tricked by his own kind to dig up drugs. And now he'd take the blame. He wouldn't give up Coyote Joe, not out of loyalty but because he wasn't a rat. He'd go with the deputy, if he had to die to give Pyen the ability to recognize trouble, so be it. This dangerous, white man was indestructible. He had eyes everywhere, and the power to imprison and kill. Besides, if Jimmy looked deep enough, he deserved it. He'd been responsible for the death of so many. Justice demanded this moment from him.

He joined the deputy outside. The big Ford loomed like a hearse. Jimmy opened the side door and stepped up into the passenger seat. With his hair loose, he pulled it to the side to buckle himself in for the ride. A few days ago, he could have taken this truck and driven straight to the reservation with Pyen by his side. She would be both angry and safe. But, no, he didn't think of that, instead, he and his crazy ideas would put him in jail. Or worse.

"I don't like lying to your mother." The sheriff's jaw tightened. "But she would have been very upset to know where you were last night and what you were planning. And she would not like what I have to do now."

"How did you escape?"

Jimmy couldn't be afraid to ask this man anymore questions. Back talk always got a backhand, but he refused to end his life on a whimper. "I climb the opposite ridge, it took me a couple hours, but I found myself on the opposite side near the quarry."

"So why didn't you tell on us?"

"Once I got to the tent and saw you two boys sleeping, I didn't need to set off any alarms."

Creepy. Jimmy shivered. The idea of this man watching him in such a vulnerable position made him want to puke.

"How did you know about the Monument?"

"I read the note."

Jimmy didn't say anything.

"I wadded the Taco Bell bag up and put it in your drawer. Coyote Joe placed the note on your bed after he stole your PlayStation. I needed the evidence to put the drug addict away for good."

"You knew he sent me to dig up drugs." He felt played.

"Yup."

"So, you used me."

"I had to."

"So, you don't care about me or my mother at all."

"I care about you both, more than you know."

Yuck. That wasn't the response he expected. The idea of the deputy really caring for Pyen was just as gross as the demon manipulating her. Jimmy wanted her away from white men. He fought back the nausea as the deputy stopped on the corner of 500 East and Highway 40. They drove past the dinosaur museum. It seemed like forever ago when he thought he'd be back to see the big skeleton inside. It hurt his heart. Vernal and its grumpy people held some missed potential now that Jimmy was about to lose them. They passed the police station, the current home of the crafty crackhead who pretended to be his friend, arrested by the whack-job deputy. He didn't want to talk to that jerk any more, especially not on his way to jail. They passed the war memorial and library. It wasn't until they'd gotten all the way to Taco Bell that he realized that the deputy wasn't turning around.

The blue skyline hung steady over the horizon as desert rocks sped past beneath it. The sublime sensation calmed him. Every day the earth moved, but nothing really changed. The calm fact replaced the fear he'd run away from for a lifetime. As the deputy drove out of town, Jimmy accepted what leaving Vernal meant. Numb resolve had replaced the pain and fear. The eye of an emotional storm. They'd come before. But his instincts told him he'd be with the dinosaurs before the wave of hurt crashed against him again.

Justice will be done when I die. It's right. The deputy has every right to kill me. It's only fair. Of course, he has no idea that I'm responsible for the death of so many of his kind. But he doesn't need to know that in order to avenge those deaths. It was bound to happen. And to be honest, Jimmy thought, I'm ready. I don't want to fight any more. In the end my death will bring about full justice. Somewhere in heaven, the beast must be smiling.

Jimmy had no idea how the devil thought he'd get away with it. Whatever he had planned, killing him would be hard to cover up. Maybe they were going to Salt Lake. Maybe a bigger prison would do. But that was crazy. The deputy wouldn't have jurisdiction outside of Uintah County.

"How'd you do it?"

"Do what?" The deputy turned his reflective lens toward Jimmy. The sunglasses balanced on the bandage making the devil appear more robot than real.

"Get Coyote Joe to break into the house."

"I didn't." The deputy looked confused.

"You had to."

"Why?' The deputy accelerated past slower traffic on the two-lane highway. "Is it so impossible for you to believe your friend would steal your stuff?"

"He's not my friend. Quit calling him that."

The deputy sighed. Jimmy thought he sensed regret in the man's posture. He'd recognized sorrow in his father before. On late nights. After a big brawl. The slumped shoulders of a man who thought everyone else was asleep.

"Do you know what the coyote represents in the Ute culture?"

Jimmy didn't answer. This man reached into him at levels he didn't like. He refused to be impressed because a white man went to a library and read a book.

The deputy answered anyway. "In folk stories, he's a trickster. A character that has fun at the expense of others. No one in the Ute culture would ever trust a coyote."

The sign for Gusher whizzed by them.

Random houses lined the side of the road.

Bottle Hollow would be coming up. Jimmy had memorized the entire route. But before he could get his head around it, they passed the gas station on the left and Ute Crossing on the right. The white man must know all of Jimmy's plans. He slowed the truck down. He wanted to torture Jimmy by slowly passing the one place Jimmy wanted most. His eyes stung. The hope of freedom would be gone forever.

All of those thoughts rumbled in Jimmy's stomach until the deputy flipped on his left turn signal. Unbelievable. Jimmy held his breath. Everything about this trip felt true up until this moment. Everything felt right and justified, something he'd earned. But the world turned suddenly dreamlike as the white man turned his big white-man truck into the reservation.

Jimmy could only sit paralyzed as he wondered, why?

CHAPTER 37

Q: *Did dinosaurs have a home?*
A: *Evidence indicates annual nesting locations.*

After they turned left, the truck rumbled past a sign. "Ute Tribe. Bottle Hollow." Jimmy unrolled his window. The air tasted sweet. Ute air. His air. A phone number and a list of amenities like a campground and marina. A crisp blue lake sparkled to his right. The colors shimmered and he took in a deep breath as the freshness replaced the toxic smell of cheap cologne. Undisturbed banks stretched orange around the water, no docks or houses to interrupt the beauty.

The road stretched forward toward tall government buildings.

Not US government, but tribal government.

A smile stretched across Jimmy's face. The deputy could do whatever he wanted now, Jimmy had made it. The white man had no idea how happy Jimmy would be to die in the desert of the reservation. Buried in ancestral soil. If he could pick, he'd choose that jutting mountain to be the place of sacrifice.

They turned left again.

"This is a relatively new housing development." The deputy sounded like a tour guide. Impossible. In order to be a tour guide, the person had to know the reservation very well. This white man couldn't know this place. The smell of truck exhaust broke the spell. Why did the white man bring him here?

Immature trees didn't block the two-story homes that lined curved streets. Brick houses with aluminum siding. No adobe. No brightly painted buildings. Jimmy could no longer discern any tribal uniqueness. They could be in any neighborhood in America, including any US army base in the world.

"Why are we here?" Irritation grated through his throat and words.

The deputy didn't respond. Instead he rolled up Jimmy's window from the driver's side and turned on the air conditioner. It didn't matter. The white man had spoiled what should have been the best moment of his life. Just like every other day they'd spent together, from the moment they met at the quarry to Jimmy's adventure in the Monument. The man was a thief. Like every other white man before him, another wonderful place, spoiled forever.

He tried not to care. He couldn't let this moment become his last. This land was sovereign. The demon's badge held no powers here. Jimmy just needed to get out of the truck and run. Once they came to a stop, he'd jump out. The tribal elders would have to hear a case presented on reservation land. He had to believe that.

At the end of the street, the houses were older. But still not the paint deprived adobes he pictured. Instead, ranch-style houses stood with awning covered porches and chain link fences. If someone were to turn in here, and not notice the sign, they would never have a single idea that they'd left the boundaries of United States territories and entered an unadvertised sovereign nation. He didn't want to jump until he could see a person, but the streets and yards were vacant.

The deputy turned right and headed deeper into the world allotted to Jimmy's ancestors. They didn't travel far before the white man pulled into a parking lot. A white SUV with the word police painted on the side faced the road. Here it comes.

He knew BIA stood for the Bureau of Indian Affairs. His affairs. The deputy's plan was fully revealing itself. The white man planned on turning Jimmy into the reservation police, turning his crime into complete humiliation. Disgraced by being dragged to a reservation jail by a white man. This sucked. He leaned his head against the back of the seat and stared at the roof of the cab. This was not the way he wanted to be introduced to his elders. He shook his head. Whatever. Jail on the reservation had to be better than life under the deputy's thumb. Bring it on. Drug charges were nothing. He'd get his chance to tell the Ute police about Pyen. He'd get them to rescue her.

A uniformed Indian exited the building.

"I'll be right back." Deputy Benson got out of the truck.

Jimmy grunted. He could still run. The car was stopped. The air conditioner continued to blast cold air. The black plastic handle felt cool. The deputy's back faced the car and Jimmy slowly moved the door lock to open. It clicked and a loud pinging on the dash sounded inside the cab. Neither one of the men outside moved. He looked back at the houses down the street. What's the point of running now? The people he wanted to see would be inside that building. The Indian in uniform in front of him was part of his plan to come. Jimmy yanked on the door to re-engage the latch. He hated that the two men shook hands so easily. He turned down the air-conditioner to better hear the conversation.

The word grandfather mixed with other garbled words. What in the world? The deputy couldn't have a grandfather on the reservation. He was too white. Too blonde. Too gross. People who have Ute inside of them have to carry the color of earth in some part of their body, whether it's their hair or their skin or their eyes. Something. No. There had to be another explanation.

He tried hard to hear the rest of the conversation, but the words like "left" and "open field" were mixed with the Ute officer pointing deeper into the reservation. When Deputy Benson got back into the cab, Jimmy had to ask, "You're not taking me to jail?"

"Why would I take you to jail?"

"For the drugs."

"Those weren't yours." The white man didn't say duh, but his tone implied it.

Jimmy furrowed his brow. Outside the window, the world moved normally while everything inside churned abnormally. No jail. And they continued deeper into the reservation neighborhood.

"You need to meet your grandfather."

"My grandfather?"

Impossible. Pyen never told him about a grandfather. There weren't any pictures of her parents in the old scrapbook. Jimmy must have asked her about them at some point in his life, but he couldn't for the life of him remember what she'd said.

"You're full of it," was all he could think to say.

The deputy just shook his head and continued to drive. The mountain that Jimmy imagined to be a great place of sacrifice loomed out the window to his right. A grandfather. A living breathing Ute who was related to him. His heart couldn't help but pound harder as the reality of the moment sunk in. Pyen's father was still alive and Jimmy was about to meet him.

CHAPTER 38

Q: *How did dinosaurs sleep?*
A: *Given their size, dinosaurs probably slept lying down.*

The sign on the corner read Randlett Road. The driveway contained more dirt than gravel. A beat-up old Ford sat next to a brand new one with a few guys in it. Before Jimmy or the white man could get out of the deputy's truck, a young man came from the house. He looked like a gangbanger. No tribal dress. Not that Jimmy thought that everyone would be walking around in feathers or anything. But the whole place lacked anything that felt Indian. If anything, it felt extremely white, especially when the guy leered at Jimmy more than he did the white deputy.

Jimmy scrunched his eyebrows together. This entire experience should feel different. It should be more authentic. Any young Indian on the reservation should hate white men as much as Jimmy, if not more. Especially one in uniform. But they didn't. Jimmy shrugged and got out of the car without being asked.

He stared at the guy who still hadn't gotten into his truck long enough to recognize him. Unbelievable. This was the bus driver from the quarry. The thug-like clothing threw him. No clean-cut uniform. No brotherly greeting for Jimmy today.

Instead, the Indian wore gold chains and jeans that hung off his butt. Nothing token white about him now. Jimmy wasn't impressed. In fact, the guy tried too hard. He fist-pumped the boys in the back of the brand-new Ford. Jimmy exhaled as the guy finally peeled his tires out on the gravel driveway. He watched the truck pull off down the road with the same roar he'd heard from trucks all over Vernal.

There wasn't any difference. Ford. Extended cab. Obnoxious. Jimmy could go for a nice quiet bicycle at this point. His nerves were fried and the entire day too confusing to endure.

He heard the hinges of a door squeak. The deputy leaned against the hood of his truck as Jimmy turned to face the old man on the porch. The man's long braid hung with equal shades of black and gray. The same high cheek bones and flat nose as Pyen.

"Come on inside." The raspy voice of his grandfather vibrated against Jimmy's heart.

His shouldn't feel so terrified at the thought, but the old man could be a ghost for all he knew. Nothing in the world turned the way he expected it would today. Nothing said, it should start turning in his direction now.

"I'll wait out here while you talk." The deputy tipped his hat.

Jimmy took the steps one at a time, waiting for the boards to snap beneath him. He pinched himself and it hurt. This wasn't a dream, although there was nothing very real about it either.

The screen door slapped behind him as he entered the house. The walls in the living room were gray, and not from paint. A thick layer of second-hand smoke coated everything. Jimmy coughed, then covered his mouth. Ashtrays sat next to each chair, some of them still full of crushed butts. In the heaviness of the place, however, Jimmy felt warm. Not from the room, but from the sense that this untidy, sad, little house was home. Not the kind you find in magazines or see on TV, but the relaxed feel of love. Corny. Corny. Corny. But he couldn't tell his heart to feel any different. This man was his grandfather.

He studied the place some more. These walls watched Pyen

grow up. They weren't painted the bright red from his imagination. They weren't decorated with the skin of bears or adorned with feathers. All the furniture could have been in any white home in America. The wall hangings could have come from Kmart. Nothing overly ethnic or tribal spoke to him. Nothing except the leather-skinned, flat-faced man who stared at him from the La-Z-Boy.

The caustic smell of cigarette smoke floated into the air with his grandfather's words. "So, you're Stella's boy."

Jimmy nodded. He never used his mother's name. He preferred the Ute name for Mom and nothing else. He suddenly felt ten. Small. Confused. Pyen never told him that his own grandfather was alive. He was too relieved to be angry at her. This wasn't a dream. It was all real.

"You gonna just stand there?"

"No." Jimmy sat down and watched his grandfather pick up a pack of cigarettes from the stand next to him. The old man tapped it against the box until a Marlboro danced to the top. He eyed Jimmy for a minute and then set the pack on the table next to an overloaded ashtray.

Jimmy sunk down into the worn sofa. What do you say to someone you just met who you should have known your whole life? Words were lost in Jimmy's brain. He couldn't think of anything relevant to say so he asked, "Do you have horses?" A stupid question. An obscure question. A question that a white man would ask an Indian. It just popped out.

"Not anymore. I used to ride." The old man's teeth were stained yellow. "Want somethin' to drink?"

"No, thank you."

Grandfather nodded and tapped the pack next to him. What do you say to a stranger who is a part of your family? Jimmy picked at his jeans. He wanted the old man to like him. In fact, he wanted the old man to like him enough to save both he and Pyen. "You can smoke if you want."

"You sure?"

"Yeah." He wouldn't deny this man anything. The old man lit the cigarette. "Horrible habit," he said as smoked leaked from his thin lips. Another pull brightened the red ash on the end of the cigarette.

"I hope you don't mind my saying, but you look like you've been in a battle."

Jimmy rubbed at the bruises on his arm, the wounds that were supposed to get him access to the elders were now just a joke. "Got stuck in a flash flood last night."

"I heard."

"From who?"

"Andrew. He told me you met Joe Wopsock."

"Who?"

"Coyote Joe."

"Oh. Yeah." Jimmy felt the back of his neck get hot at the sound of the no-account Indian's name. The homeless man was the first Indian in Jimmy's life that he hated and the thought of that pissed him off. Stupid jerk.

The old man spit out tobacco flakes from his tongue. "He's not completely no good. His mother and father died when he was young. He turned to drugs."

"That's no excuse."

"You're right," Grandfather exhaled. Jimmy liked the sound of that. Grandfather. He'd heard kids use the word all his life. He'd had teachers ask questions. But he never thought he'd ever have one he could talk about, let alone talk to. "Coyote Joe sold his reservation rights for seven thousand dollars back in the 1980's."

"What do you mean?" Jimmy leaned forward. The smell of smoke no longer bothering him.

"Means he lost his membership and allotments."

"Like me."

"You never sold anything." His grandfather gestured to Jimmy with the burning edge of his cigarette. "And neither did your mother." The old man wiped a red handkerchief across his face. "Joe could live with relatives, he just can't have any allotment."

"You mean money?"

"Yeah."

"I'd stay for free." As soon as he said it, he wished he hadn't. Not because he didn't want to stay in this house with his grandfather, but because he didn't want to beg.

The old man took another long drag as Jimmy tried to let his brain catch up. He was on the reservation. In the house Pyen grew up in. He was within feet of not only a real Ute, but his own grandfather. Unbelievable.

More remarkable.

The deputy brought him here.

"So, what do they call you?"

"Jimmy."

"Jimmy?" His already wrinkled brow furrowed so more. "Why would a big guy like you want to be called a wimpy name like that?"

"Simple." He wiped his hands on his pants. "I don't like to be called Jim or James."

"Why not?"

"Because that's what they called my father." He stared into the old man's eyes. Maybe for the first time in his life, he'd have someone who would understand. Someone he could talk to about it.

"Is that what this is all about?"

Jimmy shrugged.

His grandfather tapped ashes into an already full ceramic bowl. "You have to make peace with this."

"With what?" Jimmy bit his lip.

"With the white man."

"Why?"

"Because he's part of you. You're connected. You're part white. You need to understand what that means."

While he knew what his grandfather said was true, he hated the words. He hated them all. He didn't want anyone thinking of him as a white man. Outside the window, the blue sky reminded him of fresh air and freedom.

"What about that man out front?" The old man pointed toward the door with his cigarette.

"Who?"

"The deputy who brought you here?" Grandfather didn't know the fight Jimmy experienced to get here. And the odd combination of events that turned in his direction. Maybe a

185

reservation was the perfect place for a white man to take an Indian. But this devil had enough evidence to throw him into jail, if not for drugs then for assault.

Jimmy finally said, "I can't stand him."

Grandfather asked him, "So, you've decided that all white men are evil. They are all violent and abusive."

"Yes."

"And you base this on what?"

"My life."

The old man dipped his head.

"Even the cops in Vernal think he's a whack job."

His grandfather laughed, "The cops in Vernal."

"What?"

"Something you need to know about being a deputy rather than being a cop. As a cop you have backup, you only monitor a few miles. That man out there has over 150 miles of land to keep safe and he has to do it all by hisself."

"So," Jimmy fidgeted a little in his chair.

"So, you try taking down two or three idiots with guns when you know nobody's coming to save your sorry behind."

He didn't respond, instead Jimmy remembered the shot in the trailer park. A tactic to scare the bad guy. A bird whistled outside. No real sounds of traffic came in the window. The quiet he expected to find on the reservation. He just didn't expect to be sitting across from a living-cigarette-puffing grandfather. He didn't want to argue with him, and he didn't want to explain. He folded his arms over his chest and waited.

"Do you wonder why your mother won't come back here?" The old man asked after nursing the very last bit of tar and nicotine from the cigarette.

"Yes."

"It's simple." The old man smashed the remainder of his butt into the full ashtray. "She doesn't want to live with another Indian for the same reason you never want to live with another white man."

CHAPTER 39

Q: *How well could a dinosaur see?*
A: *Animals with eyes on both sides of their head lack
depth perception but have a wider field of vision.*

In the next few weeks, Jimmy found out enough about
Pyen's childhood to know what his grandfather meant. While
the abuse wasn't as harsh as what Jimmy had experienced, it
was both verbal and physical. According to his grandfather, it
was probably why she attracted violent men.

"I've been to some meetings," the old man had said. "Some
of these young men are helping us break traditions that have
nothing to do with our ancestry. Violence. Alcohol. You know,
I've learned some things."

Today was the day Pyen would become the bravest person
in the world. For the first time in almost twenty years, she was
about to face the living monster from her past. From the back
seat Jimmy saw his mother reach across and touch Deputy
Benson's shoulder. They all headed to the Fourth-of-July
powwow. Devin was in Salt Lake at a big firework show and
couldn't come. I Jimmy reassured him that there'd be more
powwow's in the future.

The truck roared through Vernal with the festive spirit
Independence Day should reflect. Through the backseat

window, the Utah sun baked his arm. It triggered a memory of when he was about four years old. His father carried him on his shoulders so he could watch a parade. He caught candy from a clown and his father laughed. They ate barbeque at the home of an officer on base, lighted sparklers and store-bought fireworks.

As the dry desert passed him by, he couldn't remember any violence on that long-ago holiday. Laughs. Smiles. Fun. The confusing blend that had always been his life.

His new life involved driving to the reservation every weekend with Deputy Benson. He still didn't like the white man, but he could stand it now without wanting to vomit.

The deputy wasn't dangerous. Crazy, but not dangerous. His behavior matched that of most men who have to patrol vast miles of land alone without backup. According to the deputy, cops didn't understand verbal judo the way a lone deputy did. The shot he'd fired outside the trailer was intended to make the person inside believe the deputy had all the power. Jimmy also learned the smoke alarm was a smoke alarm. Not a hidden camera. Pyen mounted it on the wall because she was too short to reach the ceiling. The fire in Puyallup had scared her.

"Are you excited, Paa." She peered over her shoulder at him.

"Yeah." He nodded and smiled. "I am." He turned seventeen in a couple of months, but today he felt like the four-year-old from his memory. He wouldn't fit on anyone's shoulders, but he had store-bought fireworks in a plastic bag next to him, complete with sparklers. A smile spread across his face and he didn't try to stop it. The idea of going to his first powwow had a lot to do with it.

He looked at Pyen and noticed the tightened veins on his mother's neck. "What about you?"

She shrugged. "You and Andrew will be with me."

Jimmy squeezed her shoulder. It made sense. Even with the happy memory circling his brain, if his father was alive and they were about to meet he'd be scared to see him. And while he knew his grandfather had learned a lot it could never fully lift the burden. PTSD was no joke.

The deputy turned left at Ute Petroleum.

Cars and campers littered the grass at the powwow site. A

handful of tall teepees stood among the Winnebagos. Before he got out of the car, he could feel the air tingle with excitement. Joy mixed with fun mixed with familiarity. Not his, not yet, but he was here. Really here. In the background, he could hear the pounding of drums and the loud cries in an ancient tongue. An announcer welcomed the teen boys to the field.

When he crawled out of the extended cab, the aroma of barbeque smoke filled the air. Grandfather told him they'd have Navaho Taco with mutton. Jimmy would get his first taste of Indian food, since his grandfather ate only TV dinners. Vendors with funnel cakes and ice cream were there to tempt him as well. Even though he hadn't thought of the list much these days, he still avoided sweets. He grabbed Pyen's hand, her palms were sweaty, but he didn't let go.

"I don't know if I can do this." She stopped.

"You don't have to, Pyen. You don't."

She eyed him over the seat. "But it's your first powwow, I don't want to ruin it for you."

"You won't. I can stay and have Chet give me a ride home."

"Oh, Paa." She reached up and placed her hand on his cheek. "You've gotten so big." She straightened her back and wiped her hands on her dress. "I need to see him. I need to do this." She signaled to Andrew that she was ready to go, and he hurried out to open her door.

Jimmy squeezed her hand. He didn't know if she tried to convince him or herself, but he was still proud of her.

"I don't know if he's changed or not. But I have." And she had. She'd come back to Utah with a different mindset than when they left Washington. He had missed her transformation after the fire. Guilt kept him too preoccupied to realize, she'd found the strength to be free. Even though she still chose to be with white men, specifically Deputy Benson she said, "The only power my father has over me, is the power I give him. Today, I'm going to stop giving him that."

Deputy Benson opened her door and Jimmy climbed out as well. He followed his mother across the dirt road and gave her a big hug from behind. She couldn't give him a piggy-back ride, but the idea stuck with him and he started to laugh.

The deputy tagged behind as they joined the crowds near the powwow circle. The thump of drums filled the air, as young men danced in competition to the beat. Feathers covered their bottoms in a circle like a chicken. Their headdresses had a couple long feathers and stood high on their heads like Mohawks. They bent low to the ground, using their thighs and calf muscles to tap their feet to the cries of a language strange and strong. He wanted to join in. Bells jingled in sync.

For the first time in his life, he wasn't a minority. There were still white people there. One dancer he passed was dressed head-to-toe in traditional clothes, but you couldn't mistake his blue eyes and blonde hair. It jarred him for a minute. While, brown skin and black hair dominated the grounds, the event welcomed everyone. Maybe it should have bothered him, but it didn't. This was his tribe and he was home.

His first cousin ran over to him, the Indian bus driver who scowled from grandfather's yard was named Chet. He stopped snarling at Jimmy once he discovered Jimmy couldn't become a member of the tribe. The kid didn't want to share any of his oil allotments. No problem, being Indian never meant making money to Jimmy.

Today Chet wore a simple T-shirt and jeans. No uniform or gangster look today. And the truth was, the guy wore what he wanted when he wanted. The clothes didn't label him, Jimmy had. "Hello, auntie." Chet grabbed Pyen's hand.

"Hello," she smiled. Jimmy could tell it wasn't forced.

"Come on, brother, the drum circle's waiting. We're competing soon."

"Give me a minute."

He nodded toward Pyen. He couldn't leave until she'd seen grandfather. He'd spent his life protecting her, and he wouldn't stop now. In fact, he didn't mind it as much today. This balance of protection felt right.

Under a canopy of tree branches, Deputy Benson set up their camp chairs. Pyen sunk into hers while the white man went to get drinks. An MC announced, "Let's give it up for the teen girls as they come out. Don't they look lovely?" Jimmy peeked over at the circle where brightly dressed girls stood scattered around the grass. "Keep an eye on their footwork. These girls are older and will perform more sophisticated steps."

He watched in silence. His heart thumping with the drums. Knees bounced high above leather bound feet. Bells jingled and the drummers screamed. At least it sounded like that the first time he heard it, now he could make out a few ancient words. Ute words. Most young people didn't speak the language regularly, but they learned songs and words in school and from parents. Pyen had taught him a few. She patted his arm as she began to relax. He smiled down at her as she sat in one of the folding chairs Deputy Benson set up. Jimmy knew she'd be nervous until the moment she'd met her father.

He sat next to her and they watched the teen girls complete their dance. Deputy Benson returned with some cold lemonades.

In the crowd, Jimmy spotted Coyote Joe behind them. As the homeless man approached, Deputy Benson moved in front of both him and Pyen.

"What do you want, Joe?" The white man's back was stiffer than Jimmy had seen it all morning.

"Hey kid," the old man spoke around the deputy without coming any closer. "I bet you want to punch me."

Jimmy didn't answer. What was the point? He wasn't about to ruin his day for the likes of this idiot.

"Go ahead, I deserve it."

"No one deserves to be hit, Joe." The deputy said, without giving up any room.

"I just want to tell the kid I'm sorry."

"Then say it."

Coyote Joe scowled then mumbled. "You guys don't believe me." Then he straightened. "I am sorry, kid. Really sorry. Your grandfather and the deputy got me hooked up with an Indian rehab group instead of jail time."

"That's amazing."

"Well, I did have to give up the other six boxes I'd hidden around the canyons."

"Six more?" Jimmy was stunned. That was big.

"I thought they were my safety net, man."

"You're going sober?" Jimmy shifted in his portable chair, while still allowing the white man to maintain the boundary. The last thing he ever thought he'd do was trust the deputy, but here he was, not quite hoping Deputy Benson would marry Pyen, but at least not dreading the idea.

"I guess if I'm going to start telling the truth, might as well start now." Coyote Joe shrugged. "All I know is that rehab's better than jail, man."

CHAPTER 40

Q: *Did dinosaurs ever dance?*
A: *Who knows? If you've heard of*
Barney, then the answer is yes.

Coyote Joe navigated his way around the powwow circle. The music stopped. The audience clapped and whistled. Jimmy joined them, turning to spot Grandfather nearby. The old man shook hands with a vendor who pointed in their direction. Jimmy heard Pyen gasp.

"Breathe," he whispered to her.

Her shoulders lifted as she inhaled.

She wiped sweat from her hands.

When Grandfather got close, she stood. The old man stopped a comfortable distance from them. He stood with his arms folded, while his face bore a humble frown. Holding tight to Deputy Benson's hand, Pyen got up. Without letting go of her boyfriend she approached and hugged her father in a quick sideways embrace. Not the tight hug of trust, but the beginning of forgiveness. The liberating feeling of loving someone who had harmed her. Although Jimmy wasn't in the middle of it, he felt the freedom to think of his own father. The freedom to bury James Maxwell Hunter's sins into the red soil of the reservation.

The MC announced the judging as the girls in the circle

stood in a line waiting. Each of them had a number pinned to their front. He had to go. Chet said if he didn't join the drum circle after the teen girl judging, it would be too late for him to participate. He looked at his mother and grandfather. No words were exchanged. In fact, the only thing he could feel in the air was tension.

From the drum area he saw Chet waving at him. He'd only practiced with the group for a few weeks, and he wasn't the lead drummer, but he was still good enough that the guys let him join as long as he didn't want any of the prize money for himself. Although he wanted to go, he shook his head at Chet. This was more important.

"Go ahead," Pyen smiled. She continued to grip the deputy's hand, her knuckles were white.

Jimmy shook his head. "I'll stay here."

"She's fine." The deputy nodded his head toward Chet.

Jimmy exhaled and looked at Pyen. "Go ahead," she repeated.

"Are you sure?"

"I'll come with you." Grandfather offered. Perfect. The tension came from his mother and grandfather being together, leaving was the most generous thing the old man could offer his daughter at this time.

"Okay." Jimmy put his hand on his grandfather's back, and they made their way toward Chet's drum group. His grandfather jerked his thumb backward. "You know they dated in high school, right?"

"Who?"

"Your mother and Andrew."

He swallowed. "No, I didn't know." His brain struggled to imagine his mother in high school. For the first time, he looked back at the white man and saw strength in his stance instead of intimidation and control. The white man had history with Pyen. This guy knew her before Jimmy was born. A tiny part of Jimmy's heart softened knowing all the deputy had done was try to protect him because the man loved her.

His grandfather gnawed on a toothpick. "They went to Union together. He was a good kid, teased a lot because of that white eye, but not a trouble maker like your father."

"So why didn't Pyen marry him?"

"Escape." He didn't want to think about any of that today. Not in the midst of his first powwow. He wanted to enjoy the peace. "Hey, what you did for Coyote Joe. That was nice."

"We'll see."

"Why? You don't believe he'll succeed?"

"I hope he doesn't!"

Jimmy stopped and studied his grandfather's face. "Seriously?"

"Yeah." The old man smirked and stuck the toothpick beneath his back molars. "I promised to give up smoking if he gave up the meth. I'm dying for a cigarette right now."

Wow. Given the condition of grandfather's house, an even trade. He had even more reason to root for their success.

"Let's get snow cones."

"No, I can't." He was tempted. The fair-like atmosphere pulled his thoughts back to days of funnel cakes and cotton candy. Once you're a fat person, the memory of that doesn't leave when the weight goes.

"Why shouldn't a growing boy like you eat anything he wants?"

Jimmy didn't answer. He didn't want to risk the happy balance with talk of lists. And he certainly couldn't stop just because this part of his life seemed to be working out alright. Could he? The war wasn't over.

Under flapping canopies, vendors sold beaded necklaces and dream catchers. Grandfather bought two snow cones and a bottle of water. "Whatever's holding you back, make sure it's for the right reasons."

He nodded even though understanding the right reasons wasn't something he was ever really good at. Grandfather found them a seat next to Chet under the make-shift powwow circle. He was introduced to the group of men as a Ute son returning to his tribe. He'd met most of them before and pride swelled in his heart standing next to his full-blooded grandfather. The sense of belonging felt as good as he always thought it would. A grandfather. A cousin. Relatives at a native powwow. He wasn't a stranger, he was family.

"Hey, Jimmy." A couple of them nodded at him.

"Call me Paa." He had practiced this line in the mirror of the bathroom. He wasn't sure he'd spoke aloud, but now seemed appropriate. "Or Jim instead of Jimmy." Smiles and welcomes were open and warm.

He sat in a circle of mostly guys and a couple girls. A large round drum sat like a table in the middle of them. He'd been practicing with them for the last week. It was a rare honor to be brought into a circle so quickly, but one of the other members had been arrested two weeks ago.

"Now, you don't have to sing if you don't want," one of the guys said.

"I don't know the words."

The young men laughed. "Sing what you feel."

"Does it mean anything?"

"It's a victory song."

"Cool." He squeezed next to his cousin. Another member of the circle handed him a white drum stick with leather tassels on the end.

After the announcer told the crowd the age group of the dancers and the young men were in position, Jimmy hit the drum in unison with the others. He felt the powerful force escape his tired skin. The beat thumped, constant and simple. More complicated rhythms belonged to more experienced drummers, nothing you'd find in a white rock band, instead a steady and dependable beat.

A couple drummers began to sing. Jimmy closed his eyes. It wasn't on the first cry, but shortly after, he let out a yell loud enough to reach the part of his father left in Afghanistan. Words he never could have uttered while his father lived vibrated through his arms as the drumstick landed on cowhide. In the middle of his first powwow, he vented his anger and grief.

What he previously considered as screaming, now felt like worship. A chance to praise the God he never dared believe in. He found a piece of heaven on earth that had always eluded him. Then he imagined his father resting in the peace of a loving father, and in that moment, he never loved a dead thing more.

THE END

THE END

ACKNOWLEDGEMENTS

I'd like to thank all the wonderful people who helped this book come together over the last seven years. From Salt Lake to Vernal, Buffalo to Erie, if anyone loves this book, it is because you took your valuable time to assist in the process and I thank you for that.

A special shout-out to the rez kids in Loralee Evan's English class at Uintah River High School!!

AWARD-WINNING FICTION

LT Kodzo's first book and award-winning novel, *Locker 572*. Is not a prequel to *The Center*, but Courtney does appear as a sub character.

All that is necessary for the triumph of evil is for good men to do nothing. – Edmund Burke

Welcome to North Harbor High...where a girl can get bullied to death.

Sheridan Alexander moves to her fifth foster home since kindergarten. Her two goals are to graduate and exit the system without any more trouble. That is until she is assigned locker 572 and finds the abandoned journal of Ribbon Barber.

The journal pages reveal the endless insults and abuse flung at an innocent girl. "Sticks and stones may break your bones, but words will never hurt you."
Yeah, right.

Words of hate scar forever. Sheridan needs to find Ribbon and protect her before it's too late even if it means giving up her most stable home in years. Ribbon has a right to be left alone

ABOUT THE AUTHOR

Award-winning author, LT Kodzo, champions the edgy issues faced by young people across the nation. As a dynamic speaker, she reaches into the hearts of people of all ages, receiving the President's Volunteer Service Award for her work to stop bullying and suicide. Learn more at kodzobooks.com

www.ingramcontent.com/pod-product-compliance
Lightning Source LLC
Chambersburg PA
CBHW020647260626
47157CB00008B/2946